COFFIN TO LET

When Hubert Clagg, the unpopular manager of Fairway Flats is found murdered, one of the tenants, 78 year-old Mrs. Emily Dibbett, found it necessary to call on the local vicar to let him know that she wasn't the murderer. The Reverend Jabal Jarrett was puzzled by her visit, and after more deaths at Fairway Flats, he was drawn into helping the police with their investigation.

Books by Freda Bream
in the Linford Mystery Library:

ISLAND OF FEAR
THE VICAR INVESTIGATES
WITH MURDER IN MIND
THE CORPSE ON THE CRUISE
MURDER IN THE MAP ROOM
THE VICAR DONE IT

FREDA BREAM

COFFIN
TO LET

Complete and Unabridged

LINFORD
Leicester

First Linford Edition
published September 1994

British Library CIP Data

Bream, Freda
    Coffin to let.—Large print ed.—
Linford mystery library
I. Title II. Series
823.914 [F]

ISBN 0–7089–7624–7

Published by
F. A. Thorpe (Publishing) Ltd.
Anstey, Leicestershire
Set by Words & Graphics Ltd.
Anstey, Leicestershire
Printed and bound in Great Britain by
T. J. Press (Padstow) Ltd., Padstow, Cornwall

This book is printed on acid-free paper

1

AT seventy-eight years of age one tends to be realistic and Mrs Emily Dibbett recognised the fact that her future was limited. Well, it stood to reason. Twenty more years was a possibility, fifteen likely enough, for she was in excellent health, and ten very probably indeed. But she couldn't count on it. Look at poor Milly Waters, only a fortnight ago, playing Bingo one day and falling down her back steps the next. Broke her hip, pneumonia set in and that was that. You can't stand the things the same, they'd explained, when you're going on ninety-two.

Mrs Dibbett did not fear death. She seldom thought about it, except for occasional curiosity as to what form her own would take. The ways of being born are few — she knew of only two — but there are so

1

many, and such varied, methods of leaving this world that she could not help wondering now and then which particular fate was being held in store for her. But without concern. It was not the inevitability of her end that was disturbing her, but a growing awareness that her life was a failure. It had been pleasant enough on the whole, with an average amount of ups and downs, but nothing outstanding had been accomplished. You couldn't count knitting scarves for the Red Cross or holding a Plunket collection box on a street corner as contributing anything worthwhile to society. She was leaving no lasting gift to posterity. She had achieved no unforgettable deed which would enhance her memory in the minds of her sons or warm with a glow of pride the hearts of her grandchildren. For some time now she had been considering how she could rectify this omission and had finally reached the conclusion that the most public spirited action she could take would be to remove from the midst of his suffering fellow citizens, one Hubert Edward Clagg.

Mr Clagg was the manager of Fairway Flats, the old building in Symonds Street where Mrs Dibbett had for the last six years resided. A large old villa had been converted into apartments. On the ground floor were the flats of Mr Clagg, Mrs Dibbett and two other tenants. The upper floor comprised three bed-sitting rooms, which shared a bathroom, and one small flat. Altogether there were eight tenants and Mr Clagg was unloved by them all. Only in the present housing shortage would his flats have continued to be occupied, only now could he extort the high rents he charged, refuse to do repairs and insist on 'no pets or children'. Young Mrs Jacobs had appealed to the Tenants' Protection Society about the leak in her ceiling, Mr Hamilton had protested to the Labour Department against the increase in his rent during the price freeze. Mr Lafua had consulted the Race Relations Office concerning the eviction notice served on him when Mr Clagg discovered that he was a Samoan and that his pakeha wife had obtained the flat under her maiden name of 'Robinson'. The appeals of all three had been sympathetically heard and prompt action taken. Mr Clagg was ordered to repair the roof, reduce Mr Hamilton's rent and withdraw Mr Lafua's notice to quit. He was sternly reprimanded on all three counts and particularly warned against turning away any Pacific Islander applicant for a flat. And then . . . well, no one quite knew how it happened, but after less than six weeks, all three complainants were gone. Mr and Mrs Lafua had moved into the already crowded home of a relative, Mr Hamilton had left Auckland and no one knew what had become of Mrs Jacobs, poor soul, Mr Clagg *said* they had all left of their own accord. Then their flats were re-let at an even higher rental. But that was eighteen months ago. The present tenants knew better than to complain.

Mary Grayson, the girl whose door faced that of Mrs Dibbett, maintained that Mr Clagg owned the property himself. He must, she affirmed, to be so concerned in its profits. Tom Solley, the potter in the back ground floor flat, disagreed. — Any agent taking fifteen percent of rents and a letting fee of one week's rent from each incoming tenant, would make a tidy sum. He worked it out on paper and showed them all. But then, he had the least to grumble about, for in return for keeping the small outside area tidy, he had sole use of half the back yard and had been permitted to build himself a brick kiln. He was doing well. He sold some of his pots at the International Market and regular clients called for others to sell on commission. Mrs Dibbett knew that he prudently slipped some rejects into the acquisitive hands of Hubert Clagg. You never heard Tom Solley complain really bitterly, as the others did. But then — artists! One knew what they were like and how low their standards were. One whole room of Mr Solley's flat was used for his wheel and his materials. Mrs Dibbett had been in it often enough and seen the shelves of unfired, biscuit fired, and glazed pots. She had examined his jars of chemicals, his bags of clay and the various tools he used. All most interesting, but such a mess! His back door opened onto the yard, a few steps to his kiln. He paid high rent but it would be difficult for him to find more convenient premises, and because Mr Clagg had acquired in him a free groundsman and a source of free pottery he could sell to his acquaintances, there was little danger of eviction.

But young Mrs Martin, in the little flat upstairs, was not so lucky. Mrs Martin was expecting a baby and that meant OUT. It didn't show yet but it was just a matter of time before it became generally known, so she and her husband were searching desperately for another flat, to forestall the inevitable notice to vacate. The Housing Corporation officers were no help, for in their eyes it is present conditions that decide priority for a State unit and the Martins, they insisted, were already comfortably housed. They assured the couple that they could not be turned out of where they were. But *they* didn't know Mr Clagg.

Mrs Dibbett herself had no desire to shift. Fairway Flats was within walking distance of the city and also on the route of several buses. A one-stage pensioner ticket enabled her to shop in the downtown centre, visit her friends in the suburb where she used to live while her husband was alive, and continue to attend Sunday service at St Bernard's Church, where she was still a working member of the Ladies' Guild. And where else could she find a ground floor flat? She had her name down for admittance to the Selwyn Village Home, but there was a waiting list of about ten years, and besides, she wasn't ready for it yet. Her legs were good, her digestion sound, and everyone had to expect a little rheumatism in later life. Her National Superannuation, added to a small private income from the investment of her late husband's estate, provided her with all the small luxuries she fancied, and because she was quiet, paid her rent regularly and never complained, she would probably be left where she was for some time yet. If for any reason she *was* given notice, she could, as a last resort, move down to the South Island and stay with one of her sons. So it was not for herself that she was planning her act of deliverance.

Even in appearance Hubert Clagg was unpleasant. He was rough, red, large and vulgar. He had loose hanging jowls and he sniffed. His elimination could do only good to the world, she was sure of that now. She had been quite fair about it all. She had first confirmed the fact that he had no family in New Zealand. Then she had considered the feelings of everyone else on the premises, mentally going one by one through the tenants and their likely reactions to assure herself that she was doing the right thing by them all. Any initial doubts had been erased. No one would grieve him and humanity would be in her debt. The present question was not whether, but how, to carry out her project.

Access was no problem. His hall door was left unlocked and it was the custom of the tenants to take in their rent, in an envelope marked with their name, to place in a cashbox which he kept on a corner table. You went in whether he was there or not, sometimes having your presence acknowledged by a grunt. Often he didn't even look up.

An arranged accident would cause the fewest repercussions but would be difficult to plan. Creep up behind him and drop a heavy object on his head? Her old arms might fumble and miss the target. One could do interesting things with electrical appliances, especially in a bathroom — she'd read about that — but opportunity would not be forthcoming. A sharp knife plunged into one of his soft bits? She shuddered at the thought of all the blood which would gush out. Poison was the most promising possibility. But not the painful sort, no. No! Mrs Dibbett disapproved violently of caustic rat poison, sticky fly papers and that dreadful form of rabbit control called mixed something. Mr Clagg must be removed, but let it be with the minimum of suffering. Prussic acid was said to be the fastest poison known, but its effects, though brief, could be agonising. And where could she find any? Arsenic was easier to procure, being, as everyone knew, the main ingredient of weed killers, but that, too, caused unpleasant convulsions. She'd read in detective stories of the arched back and distorted features of its victims.

But not all poisons hurt. In the last few months there had been two cases reported in the press of death through

10

the poisonous fumes of oleander shrubs. A family had been burning oleander cuttings in a garden incinerator and had just passed out, all four of them, and failed to regain consciousness. Another man had died while using oleander twigs to feed a barbecue fire. He too, according to the newspaper paragraph, had simply gone into a coma, with no warning of disaster. He wouldn't have felt a thing. Deaths at a barbecue were not as uncommon as one might suppose. In fact the Health Department had recently issued a public warning to barbecue fans not to use treated or painted timber as fuel, lest they found themselves chewing sausages garnished with arsenic or chops laced with lead. But arsenic was painful and lead was slow. Oleander leaves would be best, but there was no oleander bush on the section and no prospect of luring Mr Clagg even to attend a barbecue, let alone tend the fire. No, she'd have to think of something more readily procurable and easier to administer.

She could do it, she was sure she could. It was just a matter of choosing the right time and the right medium.

Mrs Dibbett was meditating thus as she put on her tweed coat — really, quite nippy it was, for September — locked her door and walked down to the Central Public Library, to continue her research in the section of Science and Technology.

2

THE reverend Jabal Jarrett, vicar of the church of St Bernard's in a residential suburb of Auckland, New Zealand, sat at the desk in his study. It was a Monday afternoon and Monday is traditionally a vicar's day off. To assure himself of a brief respite he should have headed for the golf course or the home of one of his sons, but work had accumulated. Before tomorrow he must reply to the Anglican Board of Missions, accept the invitation to the Archdeaconry meeting, arrange for someone to mow the church lawns while the groundsman was on leave, inspect the crack which the curate had reported to be forming in the side porch floor, discuss dance costs and estimates with the Youth Club committee and compose an article for the next issue of the parish magazine. They were all simple enough tasks, yet he was finding it difficult to concentrate on any of them, for his mind kept reverting to yesterday's incident.

He had no regrets, he told himself, none whatever, but it had caused unfavourable comments at the time. Now the true story was spreading and congratulatory remarks being made. Not by his curate, of course. Eric Bailey could not readily condone the interruption of the superficial rites and routine which gilded the true purpose of the Church. Jabal smiled as he thought of the shock poor Eric must have experienced, even beyond that of the congregation, when the vicar suddenly threw down his hymn book, strode along the centre aisle with his robes flaring behind him, grabbed one small nine-year-old boy by the collar and, to the vocal accompaniment of 'Lead Thou me On', marched him into the vestry. It must have looked a bit odd to them all. He'd glimpsed the shocked, indignant expression on the faces of the child's parents, sitting in another pew, as they half rose to protest and then subsided. They'd thought, in their innocence, that their son was merely chewing in church, that the plastic bag in the vicar's left hand contained popcorn or peanuts, and they had naturally judged him to be inordinately fussy about the behaviour of small children during his service. The choir, who knew him better, had more understanding. Brian Smithers hadn't waited to be asked. With a quick 'I'll watch him' he had slipped into the vestry and allowed Jabal to return to his prayer desk in time to finish the hymn and commence the blessing.

After the service he'd asked the boy's parents to stay behind. It was only when he'd taken them into the vestry, showed them the tube of glue and explained the purpose for which the plastic bag had been used, that they realised why their son had wanted to sit alone in an otherwise empty pew. Their reaction had been natural — indignation, disbelief, then horror. Finally they thanked him. He hoped he had convinced them of the seriousness of the matter. He had minced no words, spared no statistics, softened no details as he described the terrible effects of glue-sniffing. He had, God willing, thoroughly frightened both them and the boy. But — and this was the thought which kept nagging at him — he had not maintained a perfectly cool frame of mind. Quick action had been called for — the boy's head was actually in the bag. But he could have dealt with the matter with more equanimity. Instead of an enraged 'You stupid little fool!' as he grabbed the child, a quiet 'Come with me, please, Jimmy' would have sufficed. *He that is slow to anger is better than the mighty and he that ruleth his spirit than he that taketh a city*. He really must learn to rule his spirit on such occasions. Though who the merry Mephiboseth would *want* to take a city? Especially such a one as present-day Auckland, which could have given the cities of the plains a tip or two in ways of vice. He felt both admiration and sympathy for the courageous woman who had recently taken on the difficult job of mayor.

At this point in his thoughts there was a gentle knock on his study door and through the french windows he saw one of his more elderly parishioners. Well, serve him right for staying home on a Monday. Besides, she may have a problem that really needed his help. He must not dodge his responsibilities. He rose. "Come in, Mrs Dibbett."

Mrs Dibbett sat down in the easy chair opposite the desk and arranged her skirt. As always, she was dressed neatly and in good taste. Her snow-white hair was professionally set. She had the sense not to wear make-up any longer and her skin, though much wrinkled, was clear. Her eyes were still bright blue and she spoke with a soft, pleasant voice. But she was not as composed as usual. Jabal saw her fingers fidgeting with the handles of her bag and her feet shifting restlessly. He came round the desk — a desk creates a barrier to confidences — and pulled a chair up beside her. "Is something wrong, Mrs Dibbett?"

"I live in Fairway Flats, Mr Jarrett."

He waited and she added, "In Symonds Street, you know."

"Oh yes?" Had the poor soul been given notice, or was an undesirable new tenant moving in as a neighbour?

"Our manager, Mr Clagg, was killed last Friday evening. Murdered. Someone pushed a knife right into the middle of his back."

"Oh, was that the building where you live? I read about his death in the Herald. No wonder you're a little perturbed, Mrs Dibbett. It must have been a most unpleasant experience to have such a thing occur on the premises. But I don't think you have any cause for alarm as long as you take care to lock your doors and windows. It is unfortunately essential these days

18

to take precautions. But the intruder who attacked your manager is unlikely to come back to the same place. From what I read in the paper, he broke in looking for money. Mr Clagg must have surprised him in the act and put up a fight. A terrible thing."

"Oh no, vicar. Quite a blessing, really. And it couldn't have hurt much. Very quick, I'd say."

Jabal chose to ignore a remark which might have been uttered under stress and would later be regretted. He said, "If you're really frightened to stay on there, Mrs Dibbett, I'm sure I can arrange some temporary accommodation elsewhere until you find another flat. There are several emergency housing schemes now."

"I'm not frightened," said Mrs Dibbett, "and I have no wish to move. I don't keep much money on the premises. My National Superannuation is paid straight into my bank account. That's the only sensible thing to have done, in my opinion, and I just draw out small sums at a time."

"You're not afraid?" repeated Jabal, wondering why she had come to see him. *Something* must be worrying her. She was not a person to fuss or panic without cause. In spite of her age, her practical common sense and quick understanding of essentials made her a useful member of several committees connected with the social activities of the Ladies' Guild last year, competent, conscientious and tactful. She had politely asked his opinion on occasion, but never before sought his advice on a personal matter. She was well able to deal with her own affairs. So again he waited.

After a few moments' silence Mrs Dibbett leaned forward and said earnestly, "I didn't do it, you see."

"Didn't do what?"

"I did *not* kill Mr Clagg."

"And has someone accused you of doing so?"

She looked surprised. "Of course

20

not, vicar. How could they? I didn't do it."

Jabal looked keenly at her and wondered if she had. He harboured no illusions about the morals or behaviour of sweet-faced little old ladies. He had, in fact, few illusions at all. Anyone who has been obliged to read the Old Testament as part of his studies has a sound knowledge of the behaviour both of mankind and of the various gods which from time to time man creates to act as scapegoat for his evil deeds. Human nature has changed little over the centuries.

"You do believe me, don't you, vicar?"

He avoided a direct answer. "Why are you telling me this, Mrs Dibbett? Were you upset at questions asked by the police?"

"Certainly not. It was such a nice young man who spoke to me and took me into Mr Clagg's flat. Obviously well brought up and taught good manners by his parents."

"Why did he take you into Mr Clagg's flat?" Surely not to view the body? That would be enough to upset anyone. The police have good reasons for their procedure but it seemed callous to confront an old lady with the scene of such a tragedy. "Tell me what happened, will you?"

"Well, Mr Solley — that's one of the other tenants, he's a potter — went in to leave his rent. Mr Clagg used to leave his door unlocked and we went in when our rent was due to put it in his cashbox. So Mr Solley went in on Friday and there was Mr Clagg dead, with a knife in his back. And a simply dreadful mess in the room. Vandals, you see. So Mr Solley dialled 111 on Mr Clagg's phone and a patrol car came along with *four* uniformed policemen in it. I saw it through my window but I didn't know what had happened then, so I went out into the hall and Mr Solley told me. It didn't have the siren going though. Mr Solley had to go back with them into Mr Clagg's flat and he says they rang the C.I.B. through their radio telephone and he shouldn't have touched Mr Clagg's phone in case of prints, but who would think of that? Then the homicide squad arrived, dressed just like ordinary people. It was all most interesting." Mrs Dibbett was speaking with animation, her eyes bright and smiling, almost as if she enjoyed recounting the event.

Jabal said, rather coldly, "And what then?"

"Oh, they turned Mr Solley out but he says there were photographers and men taking fingerprints and marking the position of the body with a bit of chalk. And in the end there were *three* police cars parked outside in the street. For hours. I think one was there all night. A constable stood in the hall all the time too, but he wouldn't answer questions. He just told us to go back inside our rooms and we'd be interviewed later. And then an ambulance came — not the

St John's sort, a special police one. And they took the body away out the other door, the one onto the side path, but I could see them going out the gate through my front window."

"It must've been most unpleasant for you," murmured Jabal politely, while strongly suspecting it had been a rare treat.

"Oh no, not at all. Quite interesting. And then later a young man came to see me and asked if I'd seen or heard anything that would bear on the murder."

"And had you?"

"No. They must've made a terrible noise smashing things but it seems it took place just at the rush hour when workers were going home and it's such a busy street, especially on Fridays. I hadn't heard a thing and neither had Mr Solley because he'd been at his kiln, using the blower. He's a potter, did I tell you? And Miss Grayson hadn't come home. Her flat is just next door to Mr Clagg's. Though it's a wonder

24

the people upstairs didn't hear anything unusual. There was such a mess in Mr Clagg's flat."

"You were permitted to go in and see it?"

"We were *asked* to go in," she told him with apparent relish. "We were taken in one by one and asked to see what was missing. Oh, the mess, vicar! It was terrible. They'd torn up cushions and thrown food against the walls and every single piece of crockery and glass in the place was smashed. They must've thrown it round after they killed him, just for the fun of it. They'd emptied all the cupboards. I know, because I looked. There wasn't one single vase or cup or jar left intact — all in little bits on the floor. And butter and food all over the chairs and marmalade on the wallpaper. I can't understand what pleasure these vandals derive from destroying things."

"Was anything missing?"

"There was no money in the cashbox, the policeman said, and there should

25

have been because Hugh Fuller — that's one of the men who live upstairs — he'd left his rent when he came home that afternoon. It could have been just a few minutes before they broke in. The marble clock had gone and a couple of silver ornaments and a transistor. We told the police about that." Mrs Dibbett stopped speaking and shook her head to indicate disapproval, but Jabal had the impression that it was the vandalism, not the murder, which shocked her.

He allowed a moment or two to elapse before he said, "I don't quite understand what you want of me, Mrs Dibbett. It must've been a most upsetting experience but you tell me you don't want to move out and that you're not frightened. So what can I do for you? Are you in some way in need of help or advice?"

"Good gracious no, vicar. I merely called in to let you know I didn't do it. Of course, he was not a pleasant man. We none of us liked him."

So it was not grief that was disturbing

her and had prompted her visit. Nor, if she spoke the truth, was it fear. What then? Guilt? Jabal was assessing her physical capabilities. It would not be easy for a woman of her age to stab a man with a knife unless she knew exactly where to strike to best advantage. And could she then have had the strength to fake an appearance of vandalism?

She was continuing, "Except Miss Wallace, perhaps. She lives in the flat next to mine. She got on fairly well with him. So did Mr Solley — that's the potter. Well, he didn't like him but he tried to keep on good terms with him. A matter of policy. He used to give him pottery that wouldn't sell as first grade. I think . . . what was it St Paul said, vicar, about what a good idea it is to slip someone a gift now and then to keep them friendly?"

"Paul did not advocate bribery, Mrs Dibbett. You may be referring to the passage from Proverbs, *A gift in secret pacifieth anger; and a reward in the bosom strong wrath*. It is a statement of fact, not a recommended course of action."

"Oh, It worked very well with Mr Clagg. He didn't want Mr Solley to leave and he didn't mind at all about the kiln. I think he made quite a bit on the side by selling the pots he was given." She rose to her feet and adjusted her scarf.

Jabal still had no idea why she had come to see him and felt he was failing to offer whatever counsel she needed. He said, "What St Paul did say, Mrs Dibbett, is *Put away lying, speak every man truth with his neighbour*." He looked at her sternly, trying to will her into franker speech.

She merely remarked, "How wise."

"Are you sure there's nothing else you want to tell me?"

"No, vicar. I'll go home now."

Jabal played for time, hoping she would eventually come out with the real reason for her visit. "That's a pretty scarf you're wearing, Mrs Dibbett."

She smiled with pleasure. "Yes, isn't it? I picked it up last week at George Courts." She spoke the literal truth. She had taken the precaution of leaving her old one on the scarf stand and had rehearsed a shocked, puzzled, 'I *thought* it felt different', followed by a brief explanation about removing her scarf because of the central heating and then a mention of failing eyesight. But as it happened, no one had challenged her this time. She could've taken a handkerchief to match. "Pure silk," she added and fingered it proudly.

Jabal persisted. "I feel there is something you want to say and have not yet told me. You know that when you consult me you speak in confidence."

She looked surprised. "I'm not speaking in confidence, vicar. Not at all. I want everyone to know that I didn't kill Mr Clagg. I'd like the police to know. Will you tell them, please?"

"I'm not likely to be speaking to them. If they question you again, you can tell them."

"Oh I did. It was the first thing I told that nice young man in uniform."

He patted her on the shoulder. "Then stop worrying about it. No one is likely to accuse you." *Could* she have done it? How strong was she? Before he walked to the door with her he took up an armful of books, so that she would have to open the door herself. She made a feeble effort, then looked at him helplessly. He put down the books and opened it for her. "If you feel there's anything else you want to tell me, don't hesitate to phone or call in."

"There's nothing else," she assured him. "But be so kind as to tell the police, won't you? Goodbye, Mr Jarrett."

"Goodbye, Mrs Dibbett. God bless you."

He watched her walk down the path and out the gate. She took a few seconds to pull the gate open but she was a shrewd old lady and might guess he was watching. Yet even if her frailty was assumed, the ability needed to open the gate or a stiff french window could hardly match the force required to thrust a knife into the back of a fully clothed grown man. Jabal was puzzled.

3

CHIEF Detective-Inspector Trevor Chambers rose from his desk in the Auckland Central Police Station and warmly gripped the hand of his visitor. He and Jabal Jarrett had attended University together and in those days their tastes had been similar. Why the fellow had gone into the Church was beyond Trevor. He was an unashamed heathen himself. But the difference in their present ways of life had not weakened the strong tie of affection between them or the memory of the happy, care-free years spent in each other's company. "It's great to see you, Jabe. You look well. But I know you never have time for a social call, so what brings you here? Why are you wearing your dog collar in the middle of the big bad city? Sit down and tell me what gives. Has St Bernard's gone bankrupt or did the curate embezzle the missionary funds?"

Jabal smiled. "I would hardly consult you in either unlikely event. I'm in a clerical collar because I've been attending a meeting of the Standing Committee in the Diocesan office at Parnell. What do you know about a murder last Friday of a man in a Symonds Street block of flats?"

"*Which* murder?" Asked Trever bitterly. "Has there been only one in Symonds Street? Do you know that we now have an average of a dozen murders a month in Auckland? That a house is broken into every twenty minutes? That armed hold-ups amount to over 300 a year? Hold on, I remember now. Fellow called Clagg, wasn't it?" He looked through some papers on his desk. "Here we are. Hubert Clagg. Apartment one, Fairway Flats, Symonds Street — is that what you're referring to? Some lout or louts broke into the flat by forcing the door, emptied an unlocked cashbox, ransacked a drawer or two, probably lifted a few trinkets and a clock, smashed all the crockery and breakable ornaments and glassware in the place, threw some food at the walls and killed Clagg — not necessarily in that order. Under the influence of drugs or alcohol, presumably. It's simple enough. Typical nowadays, far too common an occurrence. How does it concern you?"

"One of my parishioners, a woman in her late seventies, lives in one of those flats. She took the trouble on Monday to come and tell me she didn't stab the man."

"Isn't that a natural reaction for an old lady?"

"It's not a natural reaction for *this* old lady. She's no fool."

"Did one of my boys put the wind up her?"

"On the contrary. She said the constable who interviewed her was a well brought up young man with nice manners."

The inspector grinned. "I must tell Bardon that. It's not the way others describe him. Perhaps she came just to tell you the news, to share her exciting experience, a novel event in her sheltered life. All the tenants were interviewed and each in turn was taken into Clagg's flat to see if he or she could name any articles usually there and now missing. Perhaps she thought we were accusing her of stealing some of his chattels."

"I don't think so. She showed some signs of uneasiness when she first came to me but she was certainly not alarmed."

"In her late seventies, you say? At that age she could be easily upset. The shock could've deranged her a little and she felt she had to talk about it with someone she trusted."

"It's possible, I suppose. But I didn't get that impression and she shows no signs of mental deterioration. She chatters and dithers when she thinks it's expected of her. She speaks very much to the point when it suits her. At the last meeting of the Spring Fair committee she made some pertinent and helpful suggestions. And I've never seen her fall asleep during a service. Whenever I notice her in church she's alert and attentive, taking part in the hymn or the liturgy."

"And that's a sign of intelligence? All right, don't answer that. Didn't she give any indication as to why she was consulting you?"

"She asked me to tell the police that she didn't kill Clagg."

"But that's not why you've come."

"Of course not. I made no such undertaking. But she made it clear that she was not speaking in confidence, so I feel free to discuss it. Could she have done it, Trev? I don't like having undetected murderers in my congregation. She found it difficult, or pretended to find it difficult, to open my rather stiff study door. Yet I know that a sharp knife will slip easily into living flesh if a suitable place is chosen."

"That's true. It's pulling it out again that's difficult, which is why we generally find the weapon left in the wound, as in this case. This was a flick knife, not the sort one would expect an old lady to have in her possession, and Clagg was wearing a jacket. Pushing a knife, however sharp, through clothing *and* body requires some strength. So does forcing an outside door."

"Exactly. And why would she need to force the door if she lives on the premises? Clagg was apparently not a suspicious type. She tells me he left the hall door of his flat unlocked and the tenants used to walk in without knocking to deposit their rent in a cashbox."

"Yes, that's how the body came to be found. His method of rent collection seems a bit simple and trusting."

"The front door was kept locked, she told me. Only his door into the entrance hall was open and the tenants were so anxious to retain their flat that there was not much risk of theft from them. He could throw them out at any time on the merest suspicion. A landlord doesn't have to state any reason for giving a tenant notice. It's only when he's foolish enough to do so that he can get himself into trouble. So none of these tenants would've given him an excuse to turn them out."

"Your old lady hadn't been threatened with eviction?"

"Is that a good motive for killing one's landlord? I think she would've told me if she feared to lose her flat. I offered to find her other accommodation and she wasn't interested."

"Hm . . . could she have forced the outside door for the express purpose of suggesting a street gang or a wandering thug — for some weird purpose she didn't confide in you?"

"I can't imagine it. Nor can I see her breaking tumblers and throwing jam around. No, Trevor, I don't think she did it. But I'm puzzled. If she'd seen an intruder or suspected one of her fellow tenants, wouldn't she simply have said so? Something prompted her visit to me but I can't guess what. How can she be mixed up in the matter? Yet I feel she must be."

"You think she hired someone to do the job? An old biddy in her seventies? A church-goer?"

"Attendance at church is no guarantee of virtue. Nor is age. And you must know from your job just how much being a female means. As the author of Ecclesiasticus put it, *all wickedness is but little to the wickedness of a woman*."

"What a suspicious devil you are, Jabe. I'm already feeling sorry for the old dear. She probably came along to you just for a chat about it. This killing has every appearance of an outside job. The autopsy showed no other cause of death than the knife wound. I'll get one of my men to have another talk with the old lady and see if he can ferret anything out. The case is far from closed, you know. They're still going through all Clagg's correspondence, examining accounts, bank statements, even notes for the milkman. It's a long tedious job but if there's anything significant to find, our boys will find it and I'll certainly let you know if anything comes up to implicate your old lady. But I think you're worrying over nothing. How are you keeping anyway? How's the family?"

The talk turned to purely domestic matters.

Some ten minutes later Jabal walked out of the Central Police Station, crossed through Aotea Square and made his way over to Symonds Street. Some instinct, born of years of association with the problems, desires, frustrations and deviously puzzling reactions to life of a wide variety of people, told him that he should not ignore the matter. While he was in the city area he would call on Mrs Dibbett and see if she was now more communicative.

Fairway Flats was easy to find, for a uniformed policeman was standing at the gate. The building was one in a row of early villas, on land probably now owned and leased out by the University, which was gradually gobbling up all the old houses in its area and replacing them with coldly academic structures of glass and concrete. The house was detached with a concrete path each side. Three garages, of more recent construction, were in a row at street level and the rest of the frontage defined by an untidy picket fence which had once been white. Apart from the garages, which were of a standard modern type, the whole place had an air of neglect. Jabal stood for a while looking at the weatherboard walls where the paint was peeling off, the crooked fence, the gate off one hinge, the bottom sill of a front window falling away from the rest of the frame. It would have been a gracious dwelling once. The roof was still sound, by the look of it, the walls were probably of kauri, and little effort would have been needed to spruce the whole place up. Its dilapidated appearance was no recommendation for the owner. *By much slothfulness the building decayeth; and through idleness of the hands the house droppeth through.* If the man Clagg had owned it he must have been both lazy and uncaring.

The constable by the gate merely nodded to Jabal and stood aside, evidently assuming from his dress that he was neither sightseer nor reporter.

"I came to see one of the residents," said Jabal and received a polite "Certainly, sir."

Jabal walked down the right-hand path, passing windows with curtains drawn and a door with a large 1 painted on its centre panel, the premises, he assumed, of the late Hubert Clagg. A seal had been placed over the lock of the door, so the police must have finished their examination of the interior. He moved on round the back of the house into a small area containing a rotary clothes line and an aged, deformed apple tree. Beyond it, blocking further progress, was a high paling fence. An open padlock hung in the hasp on a gate so Jabal detached it from its fastening, pushed open the gate and walked through.

For a moment he thought he had come upon a reconstruction of the medieval hell. Red and yellow flames were leaping, black coal dust strewed the ground and confronting him, angrily scowling, stood a ruddy-faced, hairy monster, brandishing, if not the traditional pitchfork, at least a long-handled shovel. "What the blazes do *you* want?" it roared.

Then Jabal saw that the flames emerged from the open door of the furnace of a brick kiln and that the devil was a ginger-beaded man of about forty, dressed in slacks and a ragged check shirt, a well-built creature who would have no difficulty in either forcing open other people's doors or stabbing his fellow man. This must be the potter Mrs Dibbett had mentioned.

Jabal was not the only one to have

reassessed the situation. Lucifer had seen the clerical collar and now threw down his spade and kicked shut the furnace door. "Oh, sorry, reverend. Are you lost or looking for someone? I don't imagine you came to buy a pot."

Jabal noticed that they were in a completely enclosed space, for another fence, unbroken by any gate, bridged the gap between the house and a high boundary fence. "I came to see Mrs Dibbett," he explained. "I'm sorry if I'm trespassing."

"That's all right. My fault for leaving the gate open. Sorry if I yelled. I don't allow anyone in here because the neighbourhood's full of blasted undergraduates who could come in and ruin my pots by opening the kiln door or else burn themselves to a cinder by mucking about with the fire. I have to get up a temperature of thirteen hundred for some of my glazes and I can't be on guard all the time, so I've fenced off this portion of

44

the yard to keep the mob out. If they want a pot, they go to the front door. Mrs Dibbett, eh? She's in one of the front flats. I'll take you through my place. It's quicker. Don't trip over the extension cord. I use those old vacuum cleaners to create a draught — to raise the temp. I built this kiln just after the oil crisis, so I use coal dust. Messy, but cheaper." He walked over to the gate, adjusted the padlock and snapped it shut, then led Jabal through a door in the back of the house. "Don't wipe your feet. Waste of time."

In the centre of the room stood a potter's wheel, an old model of the kick type. The vinyl flooring round it was covered with clay. Shelves lined three walls, some filled with glazed and unglazed jars, mugs, vases and jardinieres. On others were labelled and unlabelled tins, bottles, paper bags and a variety of unidentifiable objects. Sacks and more tins stood on the floor. A sink and bench over by the window held a bucket, two old saucepans, some jars and brushes and spoons. Jabal gazed around with interest.

His guide guffawed. "You can see what I do for a living, eh? Solley's the name. Tom Solley, but I don't suppose you've heard of me. Solley's pots? No, I was afraid not. This way." He walked towards a door in the adjacent wall.

Jabal paused. "This must be fascinating work. Is it very difficult to make a pot?"

"Not once you get the hang of it. As soon as you've mastered the wheel it's routine. The skill and the excitement lie in the glazing and firing. You can never be sure of results, you can never predict the colour. Unexpected things happen, disappointments and happy surprises as well. I got a smashing blue marble mix last week — look, there's a piece of it — and I bet I'll never be able to produce it again. You can slave your guts out trying to copy a colour or a special effect — put exactly the proportions you put before, keep the kiln at the same temperature for the same time to the very minute — and pull out a drab uninteresting set of jars. Still, that's the fun of it. And any colour seems to sell these days. There's a run on pottery, luckily for me. Mrs Dibbett shows a lively interest in it all. Is she a relative of yours? She's a great old biddy, isn't she? Always busy with something."

"She's one of my parishioners," Jabal told him and took the opening offered by continuing, "she was a little concerned about the tragedy that occurred here recently and I'd like to see how she is now."

"You needn't worry. She doesn't let anything get her down, that old girl. And we're none of us overcome with grief."

"Indeed? He was the manager of these flats, wasn't he?"

"Yes, Clagg, poor old sod. Someone broke in looking for money or drugs. The usual story. Wrecked the place when they couldn't find what they wanted. Clagg must've walked in when they were in the middle of their fun and they put an end to him there and then."

"That sounds like the work of a gang."

"Could be. I don't know what the police think. He was knifed in the back so it wasn't a head-on fight. He'd have been a match for them if it had been. Big burly ape. Could be one fellow got in without him hearing, took him by surprise, stabbed him and *then* started wrecking. I dunno. A whole team of police and C.I.B. chaps were working on it. Swarmed all over the house."

"It must've been distressing for you all."

"Well, a bit of a shock. Actually I was the one who found the poor guy. I went in to pay my rent — we used to just pop it in a tin cashbox he kept in his sitting room. God, what a mess! Broken glass and crockery all over the floor — every piece in the flat smashed. And the cupboards and fridge had been emptied and the contents thrown all over the room. Jam and stuff on the floor and the chairs. A piece of meat pie still sitting on the lamp shade. Filthy mess. Whoever it was really went to town. And poor old Clagg lying in the middle of it all."

"Children?" suggested Jabal.

Solley shook his hairy ginger head. "I doubt it. Kids would enjoy making the mess and even knifing a joker but they would've taken other things. This thief was a bit selective — knew what he could sell. We were each taken in by the police to see if we knew what was missing. There was a rather nice old marble clock gone off the mantelpiece and a couple of silver ornaments I used to admire but a cheap music box was still there. Kids would've taken that, don't you reckon? Of course we couldn't tell the cops exactly what was missing. We only went in to pay our rent when it was due. He didn't invite us — unsociable old blighter — and we wouldn't've gone if he had."

"I've heard he was not very well liked by the tenants."

"That's putting it mildly. He was a thorough sod. We kept our distance and so did he. I guess I saw more of him than the others did because I used to give him a jar or vase now and then, just to keep him sweet. I found out he sold them at a price I'd never have the nerve to charge myself. No, we couldn't stand the fellow, but it was still a shock to go in and find him like that, poor old bastard. I was ticked off for using the phone to ring the police. Could've been prints on it, they said. But what intruder would be barmy enough to stop and put through a phone call? I ask you! And I admit I was a bit knocked by the whole scene. I just grabbed the phone and dialled 111."

"A natural reaction."

"Lord knows what'll happen now. It's not so bad for the others but I can't uproot my kiln and I'd never find another place to build one so near the city. Come through here."

He showed Jabal into another room, obviously used as both bedroom and sitting room. In comparison with the studio, it was tidy. The bed had been made and there was an air of shabby comfort in the furnishings. They passed through and out a door already ajar, into the front entrance hall of the house. "I leave this door open for customers," said Solley, and pointed to a printed notice on it. *Solley's pots knock and enter.* "Maybe I'd better give up that habit now. Don't want a knife in my back. Though the front door is always kept locked. Any callers have to ring the bell and be let in by whoever happens to be around at the time."

The hall was large and oblong, with a staircase up one side. Four other doors opened onto it, as well as the outside front door.

"That's Clagg's quarters," said Solley, pointing. "That's where we went in with our rent. See, the police have put a seal over the lock, so it looks as if they won't be back. They took away piles of stuff. I guess they go through it at the station. That's Mrs Dibbett's door, the one front left. Number 3. Don't get lost and knock on the one beside it. You'd be defrocked if you were seen doing that. We've got to put up with having a slut on the premises." He scowled suddenly. "A tart called Wallace. *She* got on all right with Clagg, come to think of it. Like to like, I guess. He had no right to let her live here among respectable folk and give the place a bad name. I suppose she paid extra high rent to the greedy old blighter. I just hope the new owner will have the decency to send her packing. Throw her out into the street, where she belongs. I think Ma Dibbett's at home." He turned abruptly on his heel and went back into his rooms, evidently in bad humour at the very mention of Mrs Dibbett's neighbour. Jabal's 'Thank you' brought no response.

4

MRS DIBBETT'S door was opened promptly when Jabal knocked. "Why, vicar, how nice of you to call! Do come in."

Again Jabal admired the old lady's appearance. She wore a clean apron, still showing crease marks where it had been ironed and folded. It is easy to become sloppy and careless as one ages, comfortably nestling in acceptance of the fact that the world no longer cares how you look. But Mrs Dibbett was always neatly dressed. Her hair was well arranged but undyed, her lips free of lipstick, her eyebrows unpencilled, giving the impression that although she may once have been a vigorous campaigner against time, she knew, like any good general, when it was strategic to cede the battle. Or was it, thought Jabal, that she was simply cashing in on the practical advantages of looking a naive, trusting little soul? She favoured dark skirts and pink frilly blouses, both of which enhanced her air of frail innocence.

When seated he said, "You appeared to be a little worried when you called on me the other day, Mrs Dibbett. Since I had to come into the city this morning I thought I'd see how you are feeling now."

She looked surprised. "I wasn't worried, vicar, but it's kind of you to be so thoughtful. Would you care for a cup of tea?"

Jabal accepted to give himself more time, and when she went into the kitchen to put on her kettle he looked about the room. It was as he would have expected of her — clean, comfortable, not over cluttered with ornaments but with sufficient personal touches to lend it a homely, friendly atmosphere. Her sitting room windows looked out onto Symonds Street.

When she returned and began setting

out cups on a small, hand-embroidered cloth, she explained that her present concern was only the future of the flats. "Mr Day — he's one of the tenants here, a very knowledgeable and sensible man — he says they've found out that Mr Clagg really did own the building and whoever he's left it to may want to sell, and people buying flats usually demand vacant possession. That means we'd all be given notice. I don't want to shift. It's so handy here and I don't mind the traffic at all. It's a very busy street but I find that an advantage. There's always something to look at during the day. Mary finds it rather noisy. Mary's the girl in the other front flat down here. But she'd rather put up with the traffic noise than move, and it quietens down at night. None of us want to go. You see, I hadn't even *thought* of that when . . . I mean at first. I took it for granted that we'd all stay on. What do you think will happen, vicar? We each had a bank deposit book put into our letter box the other day and a letter about paying rent into the bank until further notice."

"No one can predict what the heir to the property will do," said Jabal, "but Mr Clagg's solicitors will probably handle the estate until probate is granted and that may not be for some weeks or even months."

"It's not so bad for me," continued Mrs Dibbett. "I *could* go and stay with one of my sons in the South Island, though I'd much rather not. Or perhaps there would be a vacancy in a suitable Home. But what about the others? That couple upstairs? though of course they would've had to move anyway, and the two men and young Daphne and Mary. Oh dear. And poor Mr Solley. He couldn't set up a kiln anywhere else around here. He'd have to move out to Titirangi or Howick and that would ruin his business. Potting is his livelihood."

"I've met Mr Solley," Jabal told her. "He brought me through his flat

56

because I'd gone round to the back of the house."

"Oh how nice. Such a clever artist. It's all in the glazing, he says. He has to biscuit fire his pots first and then the real skill counts, mixing the colours and the other ingredients, all depending on whether he wants the glaze to run or craze or be clear or opaque."

"It sounds as though you know a bit about it yourself."

"He's explained it all to me. So interesting. Potters keep their glazing recipes a strict secret, he says, and some of them are very envious about one of his dark reds. He offered to let me try the wheel but I don't think I'd be very good at that and it's so messy. You'll have a piece of fudge cake, won't you? Mary Grayson made it. That's the girl across the hall. You don't cook it, you see, and she won't cook any more because she says it's submission to the subservient role of women, but I think that's just Hugh Fuller's influence and she'll get over it in time."

"Mary is the occupant of the other front flat downstairs?"

"Yes. A nice young woman really. Just too easily influenced. Well, by someone she admires, like Hugh Fuller. She works at the Farmers Trading Company store. In the haberdashery at present but they move them all around. She's a sensible girl by nature. I think she'll settle down later on."

"Who are the other tenants?" asked Jabal. "I'd be interested to hear about them."

"Oh, would you?" Mrs Dibbett handed him his tea and cake and settled down happily herself, delighted to oblige him in his request. "In case you can help them find another place to live? How kind of you." She did not give Jabal time to disown this altruistic motive for his interest, but continued, "Well, upstairs, in the little flat there, it's Mr and Mrs Martin. Cecil and Vera, just a young couple and they're going to have a baby. Mr Clagg wouldn't have liked that and they knew they'd be given notice if he found out. They've been looking for another flat for some time now. *He* works in a supermarket and he could transfer to another branch he says, if only they could find accommodation. So hard for them, isn't it? Though they don't seem to make much effort. They're not exactly . . . energetic. Almost apathetic and hoping something will just turn up without any trouble on their part. Like Mrs Pritchard, who's supposed to help with the flowers on Mondays — you know?"

Jabal did. The comparison with the spiritless, unreliable woman on the St Bernard's flower roster gave him a good picture of the Martins and it was not one which depicted them smashing crockery and knifing a manager. "Who else is upstairs?" he asked.

"Daphne. Daphne de Vere, she calls herself. Very young. She's out most of the time and I've hardly spoken to her. I see more of Mr Day. Denis Day. I really don't know what he'll do if he's given notice. He works at the University and knows all about computers, so he could get into a hostel only he wouldn't want to, would he? Being so much older than the other residents? He must be well over thirty and very clever. He's rather keen on Mary, I think — that's the girl I told you about, the one over the hall from me — though I doubt that they're suited intellectually. She's just a shop assistant. *She's* more interested in Hugh Fuller, the other man upstairs, and she takes far too much notice of what he tells her. He goes to the University sometimes too, though I don't know what he does there because he's a sort of free-lance journalist and writes verse that doesn't rhyme or scan and he's in the Greenpeace movement and the Animal Rights and he organises protests."

"What sort of protests?"

"Oh, any sort. I don't think he really minds what they're about. Just a Cause, you know. It has to be a Cause, then they march down Queen Street or sit down outside a gate where people want to get in until the police come and remove them. He says we should all support Causes and the minority groups will triumph in the end. He's a very earnest young man. Well, that's all there are upstairs. Cecil and Vera Martin, Daphne de Vere, Denis Day and Hugh Fuller. The Martins have a little flat, the other three are in bed-sitting rooms. I'm sure they would all be grateful if you could find them somewhere to live, though I don't know who would take Daphne."

"It may not be necessary for any of you to shift," said Jabal. "But tell me who lives on the ground floor."

"Only the four of us now that Mr Clagg's gone. You said you'd met Tom Solley, our potter. Such a good artist. His pots sell very well. He and Hugh Fuller don't get on too happily but that's because Mr Solley doesn't approve of Josie Wallace. You'd really think an artist would be more tolerant, but he's quite . . . well, straight-laced, old-fashioned. And you see, Hugh Fuller sticks up for Josie and becomes very intense and heated if anyone speaks badly of her or says she should be turned out. It's not so much that he approves of her or what she does, it's more that other people *don't* approve and he thinks it's wrong to bow to public opinion or be swayed by prevalent ideas. That's what he says. He takes everything so seriously, poor young man. I'm afraid he's going to be much hurt before he matures."

"How did he get on with Mr Clagg?"

"He said Mr Clagg was a festering boil on the skin of society."

One which had to be lanced with a sharp flick knife? It would be interesting to meet this fiery young man. "Then he was not upset at his death?"

"Of course not. None of us were. But he was very angry about the damage to Mr Claggs's pictures and one or two antique vases, which were all smashed to bits. That is, he *said* he was angry. He enjoys having something to be indignant about and there wasn't anything else at the time."

"It would be more logical to be indignant about the taking of a man's life," commented Jabal.

"I'm sure you know best," said Mrs Dibbett politely. "Do let me pour you another cup of tea."

"Thank you," said Jabal. He felt he needed it. After a few moments he asked, "Who is Josie?"

"Josie Wallace lives downstairs here in the flat next to mine. She's a . . . *you* know, and some of the others don't think she should be allowed to stay here, especially as she uses her flat to . . . *you* know. They're not very kind about her and they've often said she ought to be made to leave. Mr Solley — that's the potter — he's really bitter about it. He's demanded once or twice that she be thrown out, he says, but Mr Clagg wouldn't do it. I think she pays a much higher rent than the rest of us and ours is high enough. Mary

Grayson — that's the girl opposite — she's quite tolerant about Josie but I think that's because of Hugh Fuller. She's really smitten with that young man and believes everything he says. The Martins won't even speak to Josie if they meet her. They turn away if she says good-morning. Of course they don't do anything about it themselves. They just complain to other people and say it's a disgrace and that someone ought to write to the Council and demand she be put out of the house."

"Is that your own view?"

Mrs Dibbett was silent for a few seconds, then she looked defiantly at the vicar and said firmly, "No, Mr Jarrett, it is not. Of course what she does is wrong, but she never uses the hall door for her . . . visitors. She has a side entrance. In fact she seldom comes into the hall at all, except to go in and pay her rent or to drop in on Mary or me. I think that's very considerate of her. And she doesn't have drunks and there's no noise. It's a pity she wants to earn her living that way but she's kind and generous, but bitter against the others as some of them are against her. Like Mr Solley. She even got on fairly well with Mr Clagg and she was the only one who did. She's a friendly soul. She sometimes comes to see me just to ask how I am and whether I want anything from the shops. She brought me hot soup when I had the flu last year and she never says anything nasty about the others — not about anyone, in fact, and I'm *not* going to snub her."

Mrs Dibbett was speaking with fervour, almost glaring at Jabal as if challenging him to contradict. She continued, "She borrows from me at times but she's always ready to lend things herself and often doesn't want them back, though of course I always return what I borrow, and she brought in a puppy that had been hurt in the street and paid out of her own pocket to have the vet fix it up and then she advertised and found its owner and I know for a fact that she refused the reward they offered. She gave a party the other evening for some children who don't have much fun. And really, she organised it very well. All home by midnight and no excessive rowdiness while it was on. That was a very kind action in my opinion and she's a kind person. Now I know you think I shouldn't say that and you think it's wrong of me to be friendly with her. Of course you have to disapprove of women like her. I know that. You wouldn't like her yourself because of what she does and because of never going to church either."

She was wrong. In the course of his duties over the years Jabal had met, and liked, several thieves, prostitutes and embezzlers. His priority scale of virtues had simple kindness at the top, chastity was well down the ladder, and since attendance at church is merely a manifestation of some other quality, not always a desirable one, it was not even on the list. But he did not explain this to Mrs Dibbett. He merely said, "Don't be ashamed of being tolerant, Mrs Dibbett. It sounds as if Miss Wallace has some excellent qualities. Who else lives downstairs?"

"That's all. Just Tom Solley and Josie and me and Mary Grayson. I told you about her. A nice young lady but under the influence of Hugh Fuller and beginning to express some very strange ideas. Equal Rights for Women and Don't Allow the Springbok Tour — or is it Do Allow . . . ? Oh, excuse me." Mrs Dibbett got up to answer a knock on her door.

"Oh, hullo, Josie."

Jabal heard a clear voice reply, "Hi, Mrs Dibbett. Here's the screwdriver you lent me and the two cups I borrowed last week for the kids' party. Sorry to have been so long in returning them. I didn't use the cups in the end. Bought two dozen of those disposable plastic tumblers. Looked more grown-up for the kids to have their fizz in.

Thanks, anyway."

"You're very welcome, my dear," said Mrs Dibbett. "We were just speaking about the party you gave for those poor children. Come along in and meet the vicar of our church."

"*Vicar*? Me?" There was a giggle outside the door and then Josie Wallace entered, grinning widely.

Jabal wondered, not for the first time, why so many women of her trade are quickly recognisable. Perhaps they need to be, to avoid the trouble of soliciting, yet it is almost as if they were made to a pattern. Bleached hair, heavy make-up, tight blouse and skirt, high heels and a pleasant expression on a rather plump face. He also wondered why Mrs Dibbett kept a screwdriver. To prise open other people's doors?

Jose had stiffened slightly as she greeted Jabal, not from any awe of his clerical garb but expecting hostility. She looked surprised when he rose to his feet and shook hands. He guessed that she had come in to meet him for the sheer fun of it and to show defiance of all she thought he stood for.

He said, "I'm very sorry about the tragedy here and the unfortunate position you all seem to be in. I hope the new owner will allow the tenants to stay on."

"Yeah," said Josie. "Gave us a real jolt to find old Clagg had been done in. You read about that sort of thing often enough but you don't really expect it to happen in your back yard. Poor old boy. Have they caught the fellow yet, do you know?"

"Not that I know of. I think it'll be reported in the press as soon as they make an arrest."

"Rotten thing to do," said Josie. "Sticking the old fellow in the back like that. I hope they get the swine that did it."

"He'll get away with it," said Mrs Dibbett. "They all have the sense to wear gloves now and there'd be no way to connect him with Mr Clagg. It's not as thought it'd be a relative or

69

a friend. Excuse me, I'll just put these away." She collected the cups and went through to the kitchen, Jabal suspected from a well-meaning intention to leave him alone with a straying soul that it was his job to guide back onto the narrow path of virtue.

"Sounds as if she knows more about it than I do," observed Josie. "I guess she made one of the cops a cup of tea and got the low-down from him. She's a kind old soul — always making someone a cup of tea or a batch of scones."

"She tells me *you* are kind and helpful to *her*."

"Who me, Lord no. She doesn't need any help. She's very independent. Always busy too and interested in everything and everybody. I just hope I can be as active when I'm her age. If I ever reach that age. You can't count on it, can you? Poor old Clagg. Didn't know what he was in for when he woke that morning."

"I'm told he was not very well liked

by the tenants here."

"Well . . . he wasn't much to look at and that put people off. Made you feel a bit sorry for the old boy. I reckon he was lonely."

"That's often the cause of a surly attitude."

"Yeah, I guess so. Well, I'll be off. I just dropped by to return some cups Mrs Dibbett lent me. Oh, I say — *you* might know what to do. I got a problem. I borrowed a few mugs from old Clagg too — it was for a kids' party. I didn't use them and I hadn't got round to giving them back when the poor old geezer was killed. What you reckon I'd better do with them? I can't get into his flat to put them back. They've locked it all up and sealed the doors."

"Someone will doubtless be taking possession of Mr Clagg's effects before long," said Jabal. "You could just hold on to them meanwhile."

"You reckon I could keep them and just pay whoever takes over? I'm a bit

71

short of coffee mugs and they're not valuable. Woolworths, by the look of it. I could do with them, — I like their shape — only I don't want to steal them."

"I feel sure you could arrange something with the administrators of the estate or the new owner."

"They don't know yet who gets the place, do they? We're all sort of waiting for news, expecting to be given notice any day. They say the place belonged to Clagg. We were never sure. He pretended he was just the manager. Hell, we might be turned out into the street with nowhere to go. Tough on the Martins."

"Mr Clagg has probably left a will with some firm of solicitors. Granting probate usually takes weeks or months, depending on how soon the Inland Revenue gives clearance, and I doubt if the solicitors would have the authority to interfere with the tenancies meanwhile."

"I don't think old Clagg had any

family, so maybe he didn't bother to make a will. Say, what'd happen then?"

"An attempt to trace his next of kin."

"And that might take months, eh? Good."

"Who do you think killed him, Miss Wallace? Have you any ideas?"

"Someone off the street, eh? Some kids or a gang? Who else would it be, making all that mess?" The answer came easily, naturally. Josie had apparently no suspicion that Mrs Dibbett could have forced a door, crept in, stabbed the manager and wrecked his flat. And of course the very idea *was* ridiculous. How *could* she have done such a thing? So why could he not rid himself of a distrust of the old lady?

He asked bluntly, "Do you think it possible that he was killed by one of the tenants?"

She showed no surprise at the question but just gave a short laugh. "You're not the first to suggest that.

But I don't reckon anyone would do it *that* way, even if they had a reason to knock the old boy off."

"Is it possible that one of the tenants disliked him sufficiently to arrange his death without actually taking part himself."

"You mean getting one of the street gangs to go and do the job? Wow, I hadn't thought of that. I guess those thugs are always ready to stick a blade in a guy and if they're paid for it, all the better. But none of the folks here would do a thing like that. Apart from everything else, they wouldn't have enough dough to cough up. Though, as a matter of fact . . . " She stopped, wrinkled her brow and bit her lip.

"Yes?"

A few moments passed before Josie replied, "Oh, nothing. I was just thinking back to when it happened."

"Miss Wallace, if you have any suspicion that one of the tenants was involved, you must tell the police and explain on what you base it."

"Well, of course I haven't. I said so. None of them did it. They wouldn't."

"Were you in the house at the time?"

"I reckon I was. About half past five it happened, they say. Mr Solley found him. Rotten for him, eh? Just went in to pay his rent. It rocked him."

"No one seems to have heard anything unusual."

"Well, it's a busy time, eh? Just when the traffic's thickest. And there's always something going on round here in the daytime. Tom Solley's furnace makes a row when he's using the vacuum cleaners."

Then Mrs Dibbett came back from the kitchen, no doubt considering that the vicar had been accorded sufficient time to effect a conversion. Josie decided that her range of possible conversation with a clergyman was now exhausted, said goodbye to them both and returned to her own rooms.

"I hope you had a good talk with her,

Mr Jarrett. She's not bad at heart, you know."

"We discussed Mr Clagg's tragic death."

"Oh — that!" Mrs Dibbett seemed disappointed. "What did you think of Josie?"

"She appears to be unusually honest and I'm sure she is kind-hearted, as you say."

"Oh, she is. I hope you'll have another talk with her sometime. I'm sure it's not too late to put her right. She's quite young."

Jabal left shortly afterwards. He had achieved nothing. Mrs Dibbett had not required comfort. He had drunk a cup of tea he didn't want. The inspection of Fairway Flats and an account of the various tenants who were at present occupying it had in no way helped to explain why Mrs Dibbett had taken the trouble to call on him for the purpose of stating that she had not killed the manager. It had, in fact, been a wasted two hours.

Weeks later, when he thought back, he wondered whether a more alert attention to what he had seen and heard that morning would have prevented the deaths which followed.

5

"OH, come in, Daphne," Mary Grayson spoke without enthusiasm, for she was always a little embarrassed when Daphne called to see her. It wasn't that she actually minded having Daphne in her flat. It was the thought that someone else, such as one of her work colleagues from the Farmer's, might call unexpectedly while Daphne was there and think that she, Mary, was also a punk. For Daphne was in her weekend outfit. Her face was plastered china white, except for jet black lips and the black circles painted round her eyes, tapering out across the temples to form the shape of a domino mask. Her hair, today a light green, was stiffened and flattened each side of her head, but pulled up along the centre into a row of five spikes, each about six inches high, reminding Mary of the spines on the back of a prehistoric monster she had seen illustrated in a magazine. Black jeans had pieces torn out of them in places and each leg had been ripped off at a different length. A man's shirt, loose and faded, was screen-printed with phrases: *Infra-Riot, Star-Smash*, and *Drink Peanut Butter*. Her nails this morning were purple.

One day she would ask Daphne why she dressed that way in the weekends. Denis Day had explained it, in his quiet, scholarly way. 'When one feels a misfit in society, there is sometimes an urge to advertise the fact, to show by unconventional dress and behaviour that one rejects the normal accepted pattern of living. Some of these people who look so strange to us are simply protesting against what they consider wrong. They dislike what they see in the world — the materialism, the self-seeking and greed, the false standards and the class snobbery. They don't want to be part of it and one of the easiest ways to declare oneself different from the mob is to look different. Don't be hard on Daphne. To earn her living she has to dress conventionally and conform to custom during the week, but Saturdays and Sundays are her own and it is then she can make her stand for individuality.'

All of which made sense. Daphne worked in a downtown coffee bar five days a week. She was certainly free to dress as she pleased in the weekend. Yet Mary couldn't help wondering if Daphne had motives other than those Denis had listed — like simply wanting to draw attention to herself and to please Hugh Fuller. Hugh didn't attempt to explain away her weird get-up. He didn't assume any need for explanation. But Hugh was different. Hugh had ideals, vision, and the bluest of blue eyes. Hugh was Daphne's friend and Mary did not want to offend him by snubbing Daphne. Besides, what Mrs Dibbett said was true. Daphne was not hurting anyone. And admittedly, she was clean. Even the faded shirt had been freshly washed. Better to look like that, as Mrs Dibbett sometimes pointed out, than to go round vandalising phone booths or snatching handbags. No one knew what Daphne and her friends did when they gathered but you never read of punk groups being in trouble with the police.

Daphne was not her real name. She'd once admitted it. Neither, Mary guessed, was de Vere. But that, too, was her own business.

Daphne did not sit down. She paced up and down Mary's small living room. It was a drab but not unpleasant room, the room of a girl who for years had been expecting to move, hoping that Fortune would one day offer new, exciting circumstances or an opportunity to be grasped.

Daphne appeared jittery. "What's going to happen to these flats, Mary? Are they going to sell the place? Will we have to shift out?"

"No one knows."

"I'll never get another place if they turn us out."

You'd have a better chance if you dressed and did your hair like a normal civilised person, thought Mary. Why doesn't someone tell her? She could be so pretty if she wanted to, with her naturally fair blonde hair and small, regular features. Why did she choose to hide them? Mary's own brown hair was straight and worn in a short bob. She knew she was no beauty. Passable, but that was all. Denis had said more than once that she had beautiful eyes, but Hugh never did. Hugh didn't care what her eyes were like, blast the man. Perhaps if she dressed less conventionally, he would notice her more? She could try . . .

"We have a right to know what's going to happen," Daphne was saying. "Hugh says we have a right to know. He says if we're given notice we can make a stand for justice if we all stick together. Like those people in the units at Mangere who simply refused to budge and in the end the Council found them other flats."

"But the landlord there was trying to force them into a 'rent to buy' scheme. That's why the court ruled in their favour. It was all in the *Herald*. Their case was different. If we're given a month's notice we can't do a thing about it. If we try to stay on they'll get a court order to have us evicted."

"Hugh says we'll get results if we act as a body and all of us protest against the notice to quit. Refuse to go. Get a reporter to write up the circumstances. He knows a chap on television who might get us featured on Top Half. He says if a thing's unfair you must protest, it's your duty to do so, not only for your own sake but for that of all others in a similar plight."

Mary tried to suppress a little thought that a landlord could hardly be labelled unfair by wanting to sell his own property and giving the tenants in it the length of notice required by law.

If Hugh said it was unfair, it must be. She said, "We've not yet been given notice. We don't know who owns the house now or what he intends to do. We may be allowed to stay."

"Yes, but Hugh says we must prepare our campaign before we know. We must have it all ready in case it's needed, he says, then move at once into action when the time comes. That's the way to get results, he says. He thinks we should meet and discuss the matter *now*, not when it's too late. We need to talk it over because we're all in the same boat. It'd just kill Tom Solley's trade if he had to shift. And what about the Martins? Where would they go? So can we use your flat?"

"What do you mean?"

"To meet in. To talk it over. Tonight?"

"Why my flat?"

"There's nowhere else. We've got only bedsitters upstairs, except the Martins and they haven't much room and you know what Tom Solley's place is like. Besides, Hugh wouldn't go in there and Tom wouldn't want him to. You know how they fight. And we can hardly meet in Josie's, can we? Hugh says why not? He gets mad at the way some of them treat Josie. Especially Tom. I wish he and Hugh weren't always at each other's throats. But I pointed out that Tom and some of the others wouldn't come if we used Josie's place. Besides, she might be wanting it."

"For business?" said Mary. She knew she ought to feel more tolerant towards Josie. She must cast off the hide-bound conventions forced on her by parents at an impressionable age. She must think more freely, unfettered by a desire to conform. Hugh had said so.

"So it's your flat or Mrs Dibbett's," went on Daphne, "and the old lady goes to bed early. We don't like to ask her. So can we meet here?"

"Yes, all right. I'm staying home tonight." Denis Day had asked her out and she had put him off once again.

He was getting too serious about her.

Daphne said, "We thought we'd meet early before anyone goes out. Would half past six do? I'll bring a packet of biscuits and Hugh's got a new jar of coffee and we'll tell them all to bring their own mug so it won't be any trouble to you and we can sit on the floor if there's not enough chairs."

"I've plenty of milk and sugar," said Mary, "so don't bother to bring that. Are you going to ask Mrs Dibbett?"

Daphne hesitated, then said, "I suppose we'll have to. But she mightn't come. After all, it's not so bad for her. They'd take her in at the Salvation Army or in a geriatric ward. I'd better get off now or I'll be late."

"Where are you going tonight?"

Daphne laughed, her black lips parting to show even white teeth. "Out," she said briefly. Then she left.

★ ★ ★

Mrs Dibbett called in during the afternoon to excuse herself from the gathering. But she was fully in favour of it, she assured Mary, and would be interested to hear what decision was reached. It was just that at her age early nights were advisable and she was sometimes in bed by seven.

All the others turned up. Tom Solley was the first to arrive. You'd think he would at least have knocked the clay off his shoes, thought Mary, as she let him in. She even suspected some on his bushy red beard.

Then Daphne with Hugh. Hugh . . . Mary wished she didn't feel that little thrill down her spine when he looked at her. He didn't dress punk like Daphne. His hair was short, well-groomed, and he wore untorn jeans and a blue open-necked shirt. Quite conventional clothes really, which didn't accord with his rebel views and lively mind. He was handsome with good features, tanned skin and dark-lashed eyes of ultramarine, eyes with fire and sparkle in them. His chin still showed a greenish-yellow bruise from his last scuffle with Tom Solley. Why did they have to come to blows? One couldn't blame Tom for it all. Hugh was so . . . so vibrant. He was a crusader, earnest, compelling, who'd fight for the rights of others, for the freedom of the shackled, the liberation of women, the betterment of the under-privileged. He'd declared war on the anomalies of society, the injustices of the whole world and all he considered to be wrong. Hugh was . . . just wonderful.

He gave her one of his warm, intimate smiles, said 'Sweet of you to let us meet here', and then sat down on the floor with Daphne. Daphne's face and hair were the same as in the morning but she had changed her shirt and jeans for a cotton T-shirt of red, black and green squares and a skirt of mid-calf length which looked like a sack. Good lord, it *was* a sack, or had been. You could see a stamped circle with *10 kg net* in it.

Denis Day was next, neatly dressed as always, politely spoken with a hint of amusement in his grey eyes. He had a lean, distinguished-looking face, with hollows under the cheekbones that made him look older than his thirty-three years. The scar on his left temple, the reminder of Tom's only attack on *him*, was fading now. It was hard to forgive Tom that. Hugh — well, you had to admit that Hugh asked for it. But how had the stuffy, stodgy, composed Denis happened to provoke a knife thrust? Denis always seemed at ease, confident and self-assured. Mary liked him and she knew that he more than liked her. She'd been out with him on several occasions and found him a pleasant companion, considerate, knowledgeable and attentive. But he wasn't Hugh.

Then Cecil and Vera Martin arrived, a colourless couple, lifeless and ineffective. Vera's pale, weak face was puckered up as usual in a worried frown. Of course she had cause. But perhaps the new owner wouldn't object to a baby in the house. Denis had said it was illegal to include 'no children' in a lease. Old Clagg would've found a way round that, so perhaps it was good that he'd gone. It might be all for the best. Cecil Martin followed his wife in, his slightly stooping figure dressed in a sloppy pullover and grey slacks that were a little too short in the legs. There was a look of vague disquiet on his long face. Mary wished that both of them would make some effort to look on the positive side and fight for what they wanted. No wonder they couldn't find another flat if they appeared at an advertiser's door with that bleak, helpless, wishy-washy stare. If she were a landlord she'd want someone who looked capable of replacing a tap washer or digging a garden and who'd know how to cope with small emergencies like a blown fuse or a broken window-catch. And there were hordes of would-be tenants for any landlord to choose from now. The Martins hadn't a chance, poor wretches. Hugh was right. It was essential that they all stick together and make a stand and lodge a protest. And prepare for it now, before the blow actually fell.

Josie was the last. Cheery, good-humoured, almost breezy, and not caring in the least that Tom Solley's figure stiffened visibly with disapproval and disgust at the sight of her. He turned away and did not even nod a greeting. The Martins reluctantly made room for her on the couch when they saw there were no chairs left, but they didn't look at her as they did it. She sat down beside them and grinned at the others. Mary liked the cheerful good-nature with which Josie accepted the ups and downs of life. It was a pity she was what she was. One couldn't really, in the circumstances, make a friend of her.

They all had seats now, except Daphne and Hugh, who were on the floor by choice. Mary suppressed a little pang of jealousy to see them there, side by side, and reminded herself that their rooms upstairs were next to each other, that all the tenants up there except the Martins had to share a bathroom and laundry, and that they naturally saw far more of one another than the occupants of the ground floor. It was perfectly natural for Hugh and Daphne to come down together. But did they *have* to sit so close? She fetched herself a stool from the kitchen and placed it next to Denis, who immediately jumped up and insisted on her exchanging it for his chair. Always thoughtful, always thinking of her comfort or welfare. Honest, good-hearted, reliable Denis.

Hugh began to speak. He didn't bother to get up. He didn't have to, to draw attention to himself. He explained briefly why they were meeting, what they hoped to achieve, and the necessity for action, concerted action, protest, refusal to submit to being shoved around . . .

In a pause Vera Martin began to

whine in her weak, reedy voice, "It's going to be aaawful. We can't find anywhere to go. It shouldn't be allowed. We . . . " Hugh cut her short, speaking firmly but without unkindness. "It doesn't help to moan, Vera. We all know your position and we're sorry for you. This meeting is partly to help you, if we can." Hugh always spoke his mind. Mary knew that he'd fight for Vera and Cecil. He'd already tried to find them a place. If anyone succeeded in doing so, it would be Hugh. If he were offered a flat himself, he'd turn it over to someone with greater need. Oh, Hugh . . . she forced herself to look at Denis, who was now speaking.

Denis knew more about the Property Law Amendments and the Rent Appeal Act 73 than any of the rest of them. He spoke calmly, clearly and to the point, as he explained that the law was on the side of any new landlord and that, provided the required amount of notice were given, no reason for terminating the tenancy had to be supplied. Hugh's idea of a joint protest and bringing to the notice of certain authorities the plight of the tenants, could not change the law but might produce offers of help. "But we're jumping the gun. Suppose I try to find out which solicitors are handling the estate and have a word with them? They may be able to give some indication of the future of the flats."

"Atta boy, Den," said Josie, and Tom Solley, without looking at her, frowned.

Dennis smiled at her. He, too, was tolerant of Josie. But then, he was slow to condemn anyone. With his usual tact, he turned to Solley and asked, "What is your view, Tom?"

Tom was sitting erect, his hands on his knees, his ginger beard thrust forward aggressively. He looked scruffy, as he usually did. There always seemed to be a bit of clay or powder that he'd omitted to wash off. He nodded his head (had he even attempted to comb his hair?) and said, "I'm with you

Denis. Get the facts first, then into battle."

Mary herself spoke after that, then Daphne and Hugh again. Much the same things were said. It was generally agreed that when Denis had done his research they would meet again and plan a definite course of action suited to the circumstances.

Then Mary suggested she serve coffee, as some of them were going out later and would soon have to leave. Each had brought a mug or cup except the Martins. Well, they wouldn't. Mary fetched them one each from the kitchen when she went to put the kettle on. Tom Solley took the jar of instant coffee which Hugh had put on the table (and would he even have touched it, thought Mary, if he knew who had brought it?), broke the paper seal and walked round the room spooning some into each mug as it was held out. Tom was left-handed and Mary had once read that misguided attempts of teachers and parents to make a left-handed child use his right hand could bring about deep emotional upsets which affected the child all its life. Was that the source of Tom's fiery temper? She would ask him one day whether his parents had tried to force him to change.

She brought in the kettle and Hugh jumped up to take it from her. Daphne produced her packet of biscuits and threw them to Denis, who followed Hugh round the room, courteously, quietly offering the packet to each person. Polite, conventional Denis, brought up in a highly respectable family, sent to Auckland Grammar, then to University. So different from Hugh's early life but she gathered it had been far from smooth. She fetched the milk and sugar and handed them round herself, until Daphne got up and took the milk jug from her.

As they sipped their coffee, Daphne asked "Do you think Mrs Dibbett will go along with us?"

"She'll have to," said Cecil Martin, nodding his head emphatically. "It's only fair. She can't expect others to do all the work."

"Certainly not," agreed his wife.

Mary looked at them with some contempt. They wouldn't do anything themselves, she'd bet on that, but they were ready to state that something should be done. All the more reason to be sorry for them. Poor gutless creatures. What would become of them?

"You can talk her into it, Mary," said Daphne. "You know her best."

Mary laughed. "I doubt that anyone could talk Mrs Dibbett into doing what she doesn't want to do. But I feel, like Denis, that she'll stick with us, whether she needs to or not. She's a good sport." It would be Cecil and Vera Martin who would chicken out, if anyone did. She wished she could shake some life into them. Sitting there, drinking coffee and eating biscuits, like animals automatically feeding because someone had thrown them a crust and told them it was teatime. No enthusiasm, even in chewing a biscuit.

"Of course she'll be with us," said Josie. "I say, this coffee tastes different. Is it a new brand?"

"Supermarket's This Week's Special," Hugh told her. "They're always calling it something different — Smooth, Tang, Suppertime — trying to con us into buying, but it doesn't work with me. I simply choose the cheapest on the shelf. Should we wait until Denis has seen the solicitors before we ask Mrs Dibbett? No sense in upsetting her unnecessarily."

"We're all upset," moaned Vera Martin. "It's worse for Cecil and me. Mr Clagg getting killed . . ."

"It wasn't *his* fault, Vera," remarked Denis.

"I got a theory about that," said Josie. "I've been thinking . . ."
Cecil broke in. "He got what he deserved. He would've turned us out. You know that."

Mary changed the subject. "I don't think Mrs Dibbett is too worried. She has sons in Dunedin. She could go down to them."

Hugh snorted. "You don't go and stay with a daughter-in-law if you have any sense."

"There are places they can put old ladies," said Daphne. "What's the matter, Josie?"

Josie had turned a peculiar shade of purple and was clutching her throat. She got up, unsteadily, "Sorry, I feel a bit sick all of a sudden. Excuse me. I'll take my coffee to my flat." The hand that held her mug was shaking.

Denis rose and walked with her to the door, opening it for her to go out. They heard him say, "Are you well enough to be by yourself? Should one of the girls come with you? Would you like me to phone a doctor?"

Josie's reply was audible too. "No thanks, I'll be all right. I'll just make myself sick. I guess it was that pie I had for lunch."

Cups were refilled and the conversation continued. Mary looked at

Tom Solley's sullen face and asked, "What pots are you making at present, Tom?"

His expression lightened, as she hoped it would. He was always ready to talk about his work. "Just starting a jardiniere. Special order. Haven't thrown it yet. They're damned difficult on the wheel, you know. It's the size." Then he turned and glared at Denis Day and Mary realized her remark had not been that of a tactful hostess after all. It was while Tom had been making a particularly large jardiniere that he had lost his temper and wounded Denis. He had been carefully moulding a delicate decoration round the top of the just formed jar and whatever Denis had said had rattled him so much that he'd picked up a knife lying on the edge of the wheel frame and lashed out, nicking Denis's temple. He had not stopped the wheel to do it but the thrust of his own body forward had spoiled the contour of the still damp pot. He'd never forgiven Denis for that, it seemed, though he admitted he'd done the damage himself. Denis had gone out, bleeding profusely but not much hurt, while Tom turned his wrath onto his jardiniere and punched it up in a rage. Tom had told them all that himself. He was never ashamed of his hot temper. He almost boasted of it at times. Denis apparently bore no grudge, and would probably not have mentioned the incident himself. Neither he nor Tom would say what actually gave rise to the attack. She said quickly, "I saw those new dark green mugs of yours at the International Market last week. Doreen and I went there in our lunch hour. They're a fabulous colour. How did you get it?"

Daphne giggled. "He won't tell you that, Mary. It's a trade secret."

Tom was recovering his good humour. "Of course it is. I only hope I can get the same shade again. I gave a jolly nice vase of it to old Clagg. Saw it broken to bits on the floor. Blasted vandals. They ought to be hanged."

"It's terrible what they do," said Vera Martin. "They ought to be stopped. Like you say, hanged."

Tom ignored her, as one did tend to ignore the Martins, and looked at Denis, who assured him, "They didn't discriminate. It was no slight on the value of your work. They just broke everything they saw."

"Probably only kids," said Daphne. "I guess the one who got in a panic and struck at Mr Clagg is shivering in his grubby sandals right now. I say, do you think Josie's all right? I thought she'd have been back by now. Maybe I'll go and see."

"I'll come with you," said Hugh. "She didn't look too good. She might need a doctor. Or stomach powder or something." They went out together.

"She'll be OK," muttered Tom. "Too much booze."

"Didn't she look funny?" remarked Vera without any noticeable sympathy.

Denis nodded. "Very much like food poisoning, I'm afraid. Didn't she say she'd had a pie for lunch? There's always a risk in buying from a small shop — they don't keep them refrigerated all the time when the shop is closed and the heating ovens don't reach a high enough temperature to kill any bacteria that have formed."

"It shouldn't be allowed," said Cecil Martin. "They should have more frequent inspection."

"There's a twenty-four hour bug going round," suggested Mary. "Two of the girls in Shoes and Bags were down with it and the Building Supplies chaps say that five of them on the same day . . . "

Then the door opened and Daphne came in. Since her face was already painted white, only her voice showed her emotion. "She's . . . Josie's — *dead*." She gasped. "Hugh is staying with her. He's phoning for the ambulance. She looks . . . her face is all twisted up. It . . . " Then she slowly sank down in a faint.

6

"DID the police give you a bad time, Mary?"

"Bloody awful," replied Mary and watched Denis wince. He didn't approve of even such a mild epithet on the lips of a woman. She didn't really know why she had used the word — to please Hugh, who swore lustily when he felt like it, or to shock Denis, resenting his rigid conservative ideas of the role of women in society and what was acceptable behaviour and deportment on their part? He still cherished old-fashioned standards that Hugh and Daphne strove to throw off. False, deceptive veneer, Hugh called them.

It was kind of Denis and Hugh to come down to see how she was standing the strain and she knew it would've been Denis's suggestion. He was the thoughtful one, protective, reliable, sensible Denis, and he had had the unusual tact to bring Hugh with him, knowing that she was not at ease in his company alone. She should not have needled him by using such a silly phrase. It had not been 'bloody awful', either. That was a lie. The two officers who had interviewed her and the constables who searched her flat had all been polite and considerate. They were simply doing their job.

She went on, "It happened in my flat, so I'm to blame. That's their simple reasoning." That wasn't true either. They had made no such accusation. She knew she was making a bid for sympathy. "They asked questions. Lots of them. On and on. Then took my fingerprints."

"We all got a gruelling, Mary," said Hugh. "They have to do it. And they've been through everyone's rooms, not just yours. They've searched the whole house. Josie was poisoned, and it wasn't just food poisoning. They told you that, I suppose?"

"They said the cause of death was poison, a rapid acting poison. They didn't say what."

"I don't suppose they know what. They were very careful with me, too, in how they worded it."

Denis was looking at her with concern. "Mary, are you all right? I don't think you should be here all alone. Couldn't you go and stay with friends?"

"I'm all right." Another lie. She was not all right. She was sickened, frightened and utterly miserable. Her inside was churned up and uncomfortable. She was dazed, yet nervous and jumpy, her head incapable of normal reasoned thought but whirling round with notions that collided and crashed and made it hurt. She could not accurately describe how she was, but of one thing she was certain — it was *not* 'all right'.

Denis knew that. He always seemed to know. He smiled at her and remarked, "That wasn't very convincingly said.

I don't think we'd better talk about Josie."

"Oh, no, I want to talk about it. It helps. The girls at work keep asking and I didn't want to say anything at first, but once I started telling them, I felt better. It makes it seem more . . . removed, somehow. As though I'm on the side line, instead of in the scrum. Understand?"

"I do," said Hugh. "I feel the same way myself. Yet we *are* in the scrum. We're all under suspicion. We must be. Mrs Dibbett is the only person in the house who could not have poisoned Josie. They told me they think she took whatever-it-is whilst she was in your flat, Mary, but they're not absolutely sure. If the poison was in some sort of capsule form it might take a while for the coating to dissolve."

"They took away the jar of coffee and what was left of the packet of biscuits and my sugar bowl. They asked about the milk but we'd used all that and I'd washed the jug."

"The poison was in her coffee," said Denis. "It must've been. She didn't take milk or sugar and she didn't have a biscuit. I handed the biscuits round myself, so I know. I suppose they asked you the same questions as the rest of us? What did she eat? Are you sure? Who handed her the coffee? Can you be certain she didn't eat anything? How do you know she didn't help herself to sugar? And so on. And you told them what we did. She had only coffee."

"But it was a new jar of coffee. You brought it, Hugh."

"Yes, and I watched Tom Solley break the seal."

There was a pause. Mary guessed what they were both hesitating to say and in the end she said it for them. "It was Tom, wasn't it?"

Denis nodded gravely. "It looks that way. Only Solley could've given her poison at that gathering and you know how he disliked her."

"But how could just one spoonful of coffee be poisoned?"

Hugh suggested, "Someone could've put poison in her mug before Tom took the coffee round."

"She was the last to arrive." Denis reminded him, "and we all brought our own containers with us except the Martins. Josie took hers back to the flat when she left."

"That's the trouble," said Hugh. "She'd apparently rinsed it out before she started to be violently ill. Daph and I saw it on the bench, turned upside down."

Mary said, "She was like that, poor Josie. Always tidy and keeping her flat clean. I used to hear her vacuuming every morning. Gosh, I only do it once a week. But if she washed out the mug, how do they know there was poison in it? How can they say anyone poisoned her here in my flat and not before she came in?"

"There could've been a trace of coffee in the sink from where she poured it away. And I suppose they've already had an autospy. They examine the stomach contents and . . . "

"Oh, don't, please, Denis!"

"Sorry, Mary. I just mean that they wouldn't make a statement unless they were sure of their facts. They could probably tell a certain amount from a first examination but I believe it can take weeks to identify a poison. Don't assume they're suspecting you. They finger-printed us all. It's routine. And they have to examine all possible poison-bearing substances. They even confiscated some capsules I had, even though they were prescribed by a doctor and labelled by a chemist."

"And they found my grass!" moaned Hugh. "They can't prosecute you just for having it on the premises, can they?"

"I thought you weren't smoking that any longer?"

"Neither I am. I only tried it once as an experiment but I never threw the stuff out and they pounced on it and gave a nasty snarl."

Denis grinned. "Serves you right.

Did you have any drugs, Mary?"

"Only a packet of aspirin and some disinfectant cream. They took the tube of cream away and they examined each aspirin tablet, looking for the little stamp. They were certainly thorough. They opened all my drawers and cupboards. Said it was routine."

"They searched the whole house," said Hugh. "I heard Solley hollering out a protest. Look, Josie's death must be connected with that of Clagg. Two sudden deaths in one house in such a short time — it wouldn't be coincidence, would it? But that's what puzzles me. Tom had no reason to kill Clagg. It wasn't in his interests."

"We can't be sure of that," argued Denis. "He might've had a good reason for wanting to get rid of him and he's just the type to wreck the place. You know what his temper's like."

Hugh fingered his bruise. "I guess I do. But there are limits. I've got a temper myself. That's how we come to blows now and then. But, hell, I wouldn't wreck a whole flat."

Mary remarked. "Josie said she had a theory about Clagg's murder. I wonder, did she know he'd done it? And did he know she knew? He was the one who disliked her most, the one who'd want to kill her."

"*And* the one with the poisons," said Hugh. "I bet the police were ages in his flat, taking samples of each and putting them in their little plastic bags. Nearly every glaze Solley uses is poisonous. He told us so."

"That doesn't prove he did it. Who was sitting next to Josie? Oh, the Martins."

"Can you imagine them having the initiative or the guts to poison anyone? And why should they want to? They didn't have any quarrel with Josie. In fact, Tom is the only one of us who had."

Denis said, "We can't be sure, Hugh. Could anyone else going round the room that evening have popped a tablet into her cup? I didn't go close enough.

I was handing round the biscuits. She shook her head so I passed on to the Martins. You took the kettle but you had your own mug in the other hand, if I remember. Daphne, what did you have?"

"I went round with the milk jug but she didn't take milk."

"I suppose any of us could have done it," said Denis. "But what a risk! Trying to doctor her coffee without being seen! And tablets take time to dissolve. Josie would've noticed one in her cup."

"There's only one explanation," said Hugh. "Solley had a small phial in his other hand and distracted Josie while he poured the contents into her mug as he spooned in the coffee. It would have to be powder, wouldn't it? The same colour. Then I poured the hot water on and it all got mixed and dissolved together. She complained that the coffee tasted funny, remember? And asked if it was a new brand?"

Mary sighed. "Yes, I remember. Did

you tell the police that?"

"Yes. If I hadn't, someone else would have. What about you, Denis?"

"I told them too. Didn't they ask you, Mary, if she'd made any comment on what she was drinking?"

"I can't remember. It's all so . . . so absolutely horrible. I can't really believe it yet. It seems like a nightmare and I keep hoping to wake up. Poor Josie. She didn't deserve to die like that."

"Solley apparently thought she did." Denis's lips set and he suddenly looked angry. "You're right. It must have been him. But how could he be sure we were all looking somewhere else at the time? Oh — was it when Vera reached back and knocked that vase of flowers over?"

"No, that was earlier," Hugh told him, "and Solley couldn't have foreseen it would happen. He must've arranged a diversion at the time, something to make Josie and all of us look away, just for a few seconds. That's all he'd need. Think! What were we talking about? We'd finished discussing how to protest. It was just 'Hold your cup out' and 'Who takes sugar?'"

"It wouldn't help if we did remember," said Denis. "There could be a dozen ways to take her eyes off her mug and he could've stood in front of her while he dropped the poison in, so the rest of us wouldn't see. The nerve of him! Yes, only Solley could've done it and he's the only one who disapproved of her."

"That's not true," protested Mary. "We all disapproved really. Tom is the one who was honest enough to say so. He's not such a hypocrite as the rest of us. We try to sit on the fence and be called tolerant while all the time we wished Josie would pack up and leave." That was what Hugh had said one day and Mary was conscious of echoing his words in an effort to please him and to let him know she was in tune with his ideas. Hugh had so often spoken heatedly about the treatment accorded Josie, claiming that even if they didn't condemn her in words, their attitude unconsciously indicated that they considered themselves a cut above her. Mary secretly thought that people who didn't do what Josie did *were* a cut above her. But she never voiced this unloyal thought to Hugh.

To her surprise Hugh did not back her up now. "It didn't matter to us if she was there or not. Tom's the only one who really cared. He was bitter."

"And you think that's why he killed her?" asked Denis. "Not because he'd killed Clagg and she found out? You don't go round poisoning people just because you disapprove of them. This was a planned killing, Hugh. God, we'd none of us be safe if eliminating undesirables was a social custom. Look at Daphne. Some narrow-minded citizen would've disposed of her long ago. Of course, Tom does have a violent temper."

"You just said this was planned, not done in a temper."

"But it could've been done in anger,

slow anger, a desire to punish, to remove what he thought was a blot on the scenery. A result of arrogant conceit. Megalomania takes that form at times. Just because Solley is making a name for himself with his pottery, he could be developing an exaggerated idea of his own importance. It may be all tied up with the artist's craving for beauty — erasing the ugliness of the world. Poets and artists are all a little unhinged. They have to be, to produce works of art."

"That's absolute nonsense." Hugh's voice rose in annoyance. "A typical viewpoint of the Philistine. One who can't do a thing himself says the man who can is crazy."

"Oh, I forgot you write verse," said Denis good-humouredly. "Sorry. I wasn't referring to you."

But Hugh was not pacified. "You're actually trying to accuse Solley of murder because he happens to have artistic talent. I don't get on with him, I admit, but that doesn't mean

I don't admire his gift. And I'm not so sure now that he *did* poison Josie or kill Clagg."

"You two have changed sides," remarked Mary. She saw a growing anger in Hugh and although Denis appeared unmoved, except to mild amusement, she tried to change the subject. "What's going to happen to Josie's flat? Are they going to let it?"

"Who's 'they'?" asked Denis. "No one knows who's taking over. Clagg did own the building, the police told me that much. He just pretended to be an agent to cover up his own greed and his refusal to do repairs. He passed the buck on to a mythical owner. So the property will presumably pass to whoever he named in his will. But I haven't yet found out who the solicitors are."

Hugh, still flushed and angry, was not to be so easily diverted. He scowled at Denis. "If you're so damned sure Tom poisoned her, why don't you go and accuse him?"

"And be poisoned for my interest? No, thank you."

"He might simply stab you again," said Mary. "You know, he could've killed you that time. There's a big artery in your temple, isn't there? Perhaps he meant to kill you, Denis."

Denis shook his head. "I doubt if he even meant to touch me. Don't blame the poor man too much for lashing out. I annoyed him and I don't resent his getting mad, it was the way he did it that offended me. He didn't even stop his work on the wheel, he just picked up a knife and thrust out with it as if I were a wasp or some other pest that had to be absent-mindedly got rid of while he worked."

"You never told us what you said to annoy him."

"That's beside the point. It wasn't until he knocked against his big pot and spoiled the shape that he really lost control of himself and I suppose one can hardly blame him — all that work gone for nothing. I lost no time in getting out. I had blood pouring down my cheek but he cared nothing about that. He was staring at the decoration he'd been doing and yelling 'I'll have to start the whole bloody thing again' and then he began breaking up the jar. I was really sorry for him."

"He's probably thoroughly ashamed of his behaviour by now," said Mary, "but you see, the same sort of thing could've happened with Mr Clagg and Josie found out, so had to be killed."

"Well go on, then," growled Hugh. "Go and ask him."

"It's too dangerous."

"Actually, it's not a bad suggestion," said Denis. "Not to accuse him, but to go and discuss it with him. If we talk about it he may give himself away."

"He would't be such a fool," snorted Hugh.

"I don't know about that," said Mary. "I think if you've killed two people you must feel awfully upset and he may say things to us that he doesn't mean to. Like letting on some reason for wanting to get rid of Mr Clagg. It would be interesting to hear him talk and we ought to be safe if we all go together."

"And if we refuse a cup of coffee," added Denis. "But what's our excuse for calling?"

"To talk it over," said Mary. "What more natural in the circs?"

Denis looked doubtful. "Well, both of you remember that. No rash accusations. Come on, then. We'll just knock and walk in, like customers."

Tom Solley was not in his studio but he walked in from the back yard when he heard them. Mary was shocked at the look of him. A beard is a useful cover for emotions but it cannot hide tired, puffy eyes. Tom had not had much sleep the night before.

"What do you want?" he growled.

Mary went straight to the point. "Tom, what do you think happened to Josie? Have you any idea?"

"Why ask me? You reckon I'm the one who knows? You've come in here to accuse me of poisoning her."

"No, of course not," chorused his three visitors, and then felt a little embarrassed since that was more or less what they *had* come for. "But we wondered how you were," said Mary. "Have the police accused you because you spooned out the coffee?"

"And she didn't take milk or sugar and she didn't have a biscuit and I have a roomful of poisons. I know, I know. Sit down," he added a little more graciously and waved to some packing cases. "No, the police haven't actually accused me. But I've been taken to the central police station and signed a statement there. Not the one they would've liked me to sign, but they didn't bully me. They can bide their time. They've taken a sample of every ingredient I've got here. Did you know, they carry dozens of little plastic bags around with them? They were flaming mad because my labels are not accurate. What's it got to do with them? If I put boric acid in a jar labelled potassium bichromate, that's my own affair. You'd think it was a crime in itself, the way they went on."

"Do they really think Josie swallowed one of your poisons?"

"They haven't said so but I bet they do. I'm tidying up because I may be arrested any moment. Don't go away, they said. Just inform the constable when you go out. Keep us in touch with your movements. Oh, all very courteous."

Mary said, "You can't blame them for that. We all have to say where we're going each time we leave the premises. And they have to test everything in the house for poisons. They even took Mrs Dibbett's indigestion and rheumatism tablets. And emptied all the rubbish tins."

"And discovered my pot," added Hugh.

"Serves you right for smoking the filthy stuff." Tom spoke to Hugh without any noticeable animosity, apparently harbouring no grudge now. "What about you, Denis? Did you have a cache of heroin?"

"I had a box of capsules. They took the contents but left me the box with the Repeat on it. Of course they have to test everything. Could any of these poisons you have affect Josie in that way?"

"How would I know? I don't eat them or feed them to others. They're mostly lead or mercury based and it takes a slow accumulation to kill. That's one of the hazards of pottery, through inhalation or accidentally licking powder off your fingers. They warn us about it in newsletters. I don't know the effect of all the stuff, but I daresay some would poison rapidly. There have been one or two accidents with kids. But who would get hold of it?"

"Anyone could walk in," said Mary. "You leave your hall door open. Josie could've taken it herself."

"Wallace wouldn't have had the nerve to come anywhere near the place.

She knew what I thought of her."

"When you're outside at your kiln, anyone could help himself. So even if the police find out that the poison Josie took was the same as something you stock, they can't say you put it in her coffee."

"Huh! Can't they? I know anyone could come in and steal the stuff but why would they? They wouldn't know what to take. And how could they give it to Wallace? I was the only one who could've done that. I didn't poison the slut. If I'd decided to knock her off I'd've used my bare hands. One of those coppers had the nerve to suggest that I might not've fired a mug properly and the glaze was still soluble. They don't know what they're talking about. I've been making and selling pottery for over ten years. Silly fools. *Me*, not fire properly? Anyway, she wasn't using one of my mugs. I'll give the police their due. They did admit she could've taken some dope before she came to your flat that evening, Mary. They said they're working on that angle. Didn't like to accuse me outright. Mustn't frighten the suspect. He might run away. They even took my fingerprints."

Denis said, "I think you're worrying before you need to, Tom. When they've identified the poison, you may find it's nothing you use. They're still working in her flat. Going over every inch. And they fingerprinted us all. It's routine. They do have a hell of a job, don't they?"

"There are plenty of them to do it. They've got a cop out the back as well as the front now, and I have to leave my gate open. He says *he'll* stop any intruders, so I don't need it locked. What he means is, he's been told to keep a constant eye on me."

Mary felt sorry for Tom as she looked at his tired eyes. Whether he'd killed two tenants or not, he was going through hell. "Cheer up, Tom. It's not as bad as you make out."

"And what's going to happen to the flats?"

"Denis is going to see the solicitors who are handling the estate. There's a good chance we'll be left alone for a while."

"Oh, I suppose so," said Tom wearily. "I shan't need a flat if I'm in jail, anyway. Coffee? I'm just going to make some."

"No thank you. We must go." If Mary's answer came a little quickly, Tom showed no sign of noticing it.

7

THREE days later detectives were still moving in and out of the house. Police cars were parked in the street most of the day and a constable stood by the front gate, turning away sightseers and reporters, and questioning all legitimate visitors before allowing them through. Each tenant had to state his intended destination when he left the premises.

Mary's rooms had been thoroughly examined, her small kitchenette in particular turned upside down and inside out. There had even been mention of sealing up her flat and finding alternative accommodation for her, but that idea had apparently been discarded. Josie had not died in her sitting room, she had merely swallowed the lethal dose while there. The C.I.B. men remained polite. They did not bully, threaten or intimidate. They did not hint that any person might be withholding guilty knowledge. But quietly, persistently, they kept on questioning. And — an ominous sign — they refused Mrs Dibbett's offers of tea and scones.

A second constable roamed the section, sometimes watching Tom Solley at work, sometimes acting as messenger or rouseabout for the detectives. Tom continued making and firing pots. The other tenants kept out of his way but among them was developing a new camaraderie. They tended to meet and chat more often than before, finding that discussion of the two deaths offered some relief for pent-up fears and emotions. Even the Martins joined in. But if Tom Solley approached a group the talk was suddenly of the weather or the city bus drivers' stop-work meeting or the rise in the price of tinned apricots.

On the Saturday morning a week after Josie's death, Daphne, Denis,

Hugh and Mary sat in Mary's sitting room.

"They'll arrest him soon," remarked Denis. "They must know he's guilty but before they take him in they have to accumulate sufficient evidence."

"How can they?" asked Mary. "There isn't any."

"Tom is left-handed and it may be possible for the pathologist to tell from the direction of the stroke that killed Clagg whether the wound was made by a right-handed or left-handed person. That's one thing. Then the forensic chemists will still be testing for the poison that killed Josie. When the police get the final lab reports, they'll be in a position to charge him. They can't do it merely on suspicion."

"We can't assume the results will incriminate him," said Hugh.

Daphne snorted. "Of course they will. He's the only one with a temper bad enough to smash up Clagg's flat." Mary thought how nice she looked in conventional dress, with a moderate amount of make-up and her blond hair brushed. Before she went out later she would convert herself into a grotesque freak.

"I don't know about that," objected Hugh. "I've got a temper myself but it doesn't run to throwing all the contents of someone's cupboards against the walls. A few plates would relieve my feelings, and I think that would have been enough for Tom too. The mess in Clagg's room looked more like vandalism by a street gang."

"I suppose he meant it to," said Daphne. "And your temper is nothing like his. He gets really beside himself at times. And what's more, he's been in prison. He told me once."

"What?" gasped Mary. "He murdered someone else?"

"If he did, he didn't tell me. He said he stole some money when he was much younger. That would've brought him only a fine or probation but the owner came in before he got away and tried to stop him getting out the window.

They had a struggle. Tom was stronger and knocked the other chap senseless. In the meantime some neighbours had heard the noise and phoned the police. Tom could've escaped but he says he didn't know how badly the fellow was hurt and couldn't very well leave him. He was trying to bring him round when the police walked in. It was called 'aggravated robbery' and he got six months."

"That's *his* version," sneered Hugh. "Made up to sound good."

Daphne said, "I can imagine him sticking a knife in old Clagg and I can even imagine him wrecking the room, but Josie wasn't poisoned in a fit of temper. That must've been planned beforehand."

"That doesn't exonerate him," argued Hugh. "Prison embitters a man. Hate and fear fester in those surroundings. Confinement breeds resentment and an urge for revenge." He leaned forward, gesticulating, his dark hair tousled, his cheeks flushed. "Don't you realise

132

what it's like? What it does to a person? Cut off from the world and not knowing what's happening to his wife and kids?"

"Tom didn't have a wife and kids," Daphne pointed out.

Hugh ignored this. "We've heard first-hand accounts of conditions at the Prison Reform League meetings. The whole system is outdated, barbarian, and fosters further crime. Guards can do as they please and get away with it. A complaint to the Governor brings retaliation in the form of increased brutality. In that unnatural environment you have nothing to do except feed your hate and plan how to take revenge against the world when you get out."

Denis laughed at him. "So Solley nurtured his hate for ten years or so and then relieved it by poisoning a next-door neighbour. What nonsense, Hugh! You have a quite distorted idea of prison life."

But Hugh was thoroughly roused by

133

now. He stood up. "What do *you* know about it? You're a typical example of the uncaring society that puts men there. You don't really care about them. Poke them out of the way, that's your remedy. Throw them into a den of hopeless misery to kill their initiative and crush their spirit. As long as they're not around to bother *you* any more, what else matters? Excuse me, I'm going." He left the room, shutting the door behind him with a little more force than necessary.

Daphne gave a nervous little giggle. "Now you've really upset him."

Mary said. "It's only that he feels things deeply. He's always thinking of the plight of someone else rather than himself." Then she saw Daphne looking at her with an amused expression and added hastily, "But he did get his hair in a knot, didn't he? Is prison really as bad as all that?"

It was Denis who answered. "No, it is not. Poor old Hugh's upset, as we all are, and was just letting off steam. Prison can be a friendly community with a good working relationship between prisoners and guards. Crafts and other interests and education are all catered for, tutors brought in, correspondence courses arranged, hobbies encouraged. If a man shows real artistic talent he may even be allotted a room as a studio. And warders are no longer uneducated brutes. They're carefully selected and trained."

"And how do *you* know?" demanded Mary. She resented Hugh's opinions being rubbished as soon as he was out of the room.

There was a pause before Denis replied, "I've read about it and I was once in a party shown over Paremoremo. Oh, I grant you that a few years of it might drive a highly sensitive person to lunacy. Someone like Hugh himself, for instance. But most inmates adapt well. The treatment's fair, the meals are good and they're not unhappy on the whole."

"But they're not put there to be

happy," objected Daphne. "They ought to be punished, not pampered."

"Simply being there is their punishment. Loss of freedom. I agree that crime must be punished, but those inside are given a chance of reformation. Only they call it 'rehabilitation' now because it sounds nicer. They're not pampered. Privileges are granted so that when necessary they can be withheld as a means of discipline. The prisoners know that."

"You talk as though they enjoy it all."

"Of course they don't. They're not meant to. Would you like to live with the clang of steel gates constantly in your ears? All day and all night, as workers, prisoners, visitors, tutors, warders, pass through the check points, those gates clang. One set opens — clang! — and you pass into a little cage over looked by close circuit television. Then they close behind you — clang. You wait until the front ones open, pass through — another clang.

You can hear it all over the prison. For the rest of their lives these men remember the clanging of the gates. But all the same, it's not as bad as Hugh describes it. I don't know why he got so upset."

Denis spoke calmly, unemotionally, unlike Hugh. There was no heat in his voice, no particular emphasis. Yet Mary wondered why he knew so much about prisons. Had he, too, had personal experience? What was going on behind that impassive expression? Only narrowing of the eyes now and then, a tightening of the face muscles and a slight stiffening of his posture, betrayed some inner feeling.

"Do you approve of imprisoning criminals then?" she asked, to lead him on.

"I approve of punishment, and incarceration is one form of punishment. It's not wise for a community to condone crime, yet there's a growing tendency to offer more sympathy to the offender than to victim."

"And you don't approve of that?" Mary tried to rouse him. "You'd like to see poor old Tom hanged?"

Denis hesitated and then said, "Perhaps. If he's killed two persons here he can kill again and he's best removed before he does it." He smiled slightly. "I admit that capital punishment can hardly be classed as rehabilitation, but one must consider the need to provide protection for others. Too often a killer is confined for a few years, then released to kill again. That's what may happen to Solley. Once a killer, always a killer."

Daphne said, "Hugh seems to think that it's partly because Tom's been in prison that he killed Clagg and Josie."

"But that was years ago, you said," argued Mary. "Why would it suddenly affect him now? But something's bugging him. You can tell."

"For heaven's sake, Mary," said Denis, at last showing some feeling in his tone, "isn't there something bugging us all? There have just been two violent deaths in the house we live in and you express surprise that someone besides yourself is upset. Don't forget Tom is the suspect and is well aware of it. Of course he's troubled."

"No, no, it's more than that. There's something else preying on his mind."

"On his conscience," corrected Daphne. "It must be knowing that even if the police don't suspect him, we do. That's why he looks so ghastly."

"Then let's show him we don't," suggested Mary.

"But we do. He's the only one who could've poisoned Josie."

"That's not being charitable. Let's ask him to come and have a cup of tea with us. He ought to be given a chance."

"A chance to poison us too?"

"He disapproved strongly of Josie. He doesn't feel the same way about us. And we've given him no hint that we think he killed Mr Clagg. Anyway, he might give himself away if we talk with him about it and then we'll know for sure. So let's ask him to come and have a cuppa — and I'll pour the tea."

Denis smiled. "A sort of last cigarette before the firing squad? Remember we went to see him the other day in the hope he'd say 'Sorry folks. I did it,' and he wouldn't oblige. But you're right, Mary. It can do no harm to ask him in. Of course if he's firing he won't come."

"It doesn't matter whether he comes or not. It's inviting him that matters. Showing him that the whole world is not against him and that we don't suspect him."

"In spite of the fact that we do," grinned Daphne. "All right. Shall I go?"

Denis got up. "I think I'd better. If he does turn violent I'm a little more capable of defending myself."

"Don't go round the back," advised Daphne. "He'll throw a shovel at you."

"I think I *will* go there first, to see if he's firing and postpone the invitation if he is." Denis left the room quietly.

Mary again thought how dependable he was, how sensible and composed. He had admirable qualities, all of which she admired. But how did he know so much about prisons?

Daphne saw her looking after him and read her mind. "He hasn't been in prison himself, Mary. He belonged to the Prison Reform League once, he told me. He's a dark horse, Den. Does an awful lot for other people but doesn't show off and scream to the world, like Hugh."

Mary bit back the angry retort that would only confirm her interest in Hugh. It was strange — she didn't care if Hugh *had* been in prison. She'd like him just as much. But for some odd reason, she didn't like to think that Denis had. And what that meant, she didn't know.

Daphne asked, "Are you scared, Mary?"

"Yes, of course I am. I try not to show it but I'm really terrified underneath, aren't you? All that stops me from yelling sometimes is the sort of unreality of it. Like a bad dream. And it's not quite so awful during the day, while I'm at work. Perhaps I revel in being a celebrity there now. Everyone wanting to talk to me and ask me about it, and actually, it helps to tell them. I don't mind answering their questions at all, and they're not ghoulish or callous. They're awfully nice to me. It's at night that it gets to me."

"Me too. I hop out of bed sometimes to make sure that the door's locked, even though I know damn well I turned the key. But Tom's got nothing against us. I keep telling myself that. Then I imagine I hear footsteps and wonder if it's him, creeping up the stairs with a knife in his hand. He did do it, Mary. He must have. Both Clagg and Josie."

"Yes, I know. I argue against it but all the time I know he's the one. Why don't they hurry up and arrest him so we can all breathe again?"

"I guess it's like Denis says. They don't have definite proof yet. They'll take him away soon and make him confess. Hugh says they shine a bright light in your eyes and keep you from sleep by asking you questions, until you don't know what you're saying any more and just confess to put an end to it. He says it's a form of torture the Western world gets away with."

"I wish Hugh hadn't stormed out like that."

"Don't worry. That's his way. He feels things so. Sometimes he blows his top and other times he goes all quiet and glumps for hours. He said he was going to a meeting of the Anti-fluoridation Society this morning, so that's really why he left, I think. And since we're asking Tom to come in, it's just as well he did. They could start scrapping."

"Yes, of course, though they talked all right together the other day. If Tom comes back with Denis, we mustn't give any sign that we know he's guilty.

143

We must behave naturally. I'd better put the kettle on."

"I'll come and help."

They brought back cups and biscuits from the kitchen and Daphne remarked, "It would be better if we were using some of Tom's own mugs."

"He's never given me any."

"Nor me. But he might think you should've bought some. He's so touchy. Oh gosh, he wouldn't murder you for that, would he? Of course not. I'm getting so scared of him I'm not even talking sense. You know, it won't be easy to behave naturally while he's here. What shall we talk about?"

"His pottery," said Mary. "And I'll ask about buying a couple of his mugs. That ought to please him and I shan't have to do it while he's in jail. And we can ask him about designs and colours. If we keep the talk on his work we should be safe."

"They'll be here any minute. I wonder if Den is arguing with him, trying to persuade him to come. Oh golly, I hope he hasn't said something to annoy Tom like that other time. Oh no, he wouldn't. Perhaps Tom's confessing to him. You know, Mary, I think he'll give himself up in the end. It must be terrible to have crimes like that on your conscience. He ought to own up, for the sake of the rest of us."

"And for his own. It's only a matter of time and he must know that. He's no fool, and he's not all bad, Daph. He's generous in lots of ways. I reckon he didn't realise that killing Mr Clagg and Josie would affect so many other people. I'm going to make the tea, Daph. We'll have a cup whether he comes or not."

When she returned with the teapot she said, "Now we're going to be very calm and casual and talk about pottery."

Then the door opened and Denis came in alone. For a moment he did not speak. He looked unusually solemn.

"Oh, isn't he coming?" asked Mary.

"Couldn't you persuade him?"

Denis looked at them both gravely. "Now don't panic, either of you. But there's been another . . . Tom Solley is dead."

Daphne started to scream and put her hand over her mouth. Mary heard herself speaking as if it were someone else, a long way off. "Dead? How? Has he committed suicide? Or was it a heart attack?"

"Sit down, Mary. Both of you. Is that tea? You'd better each have a cup." He lifted the teapot and poured some into two mugs, then, as an afterthought, a third. He put two teaspoonfuls of sugar in each. He knows I don't take sugar, thought Mary. He knows. Oh, what does it matter? What am I thinking about? Tea?

"What happened, Denis?" She tried to keep her voice from rising hysterically. "How do you mean, dead? How do you know?"

"Drink your tea," said Denis dully. "The sugar will help — it's the

146

recognised treatment for shock." Then he sat down himself and stared, as if stunned, at his own cup.

"Tell us," said Mary. "We'll have to know."

Denis looked up at her. "Yes, you'll have to know. Tom Solley has been hit on the head. His skull's smashed in."

"Oh hell," gasped Daphne. "What did you do?"

"I . . . nothing. I left him there. On the floor next to his wheel, where he was. The poor guy's . . . quite dead. We'll have to let the police know. I was going to use his phone then I remembered how he got into trouble for using Clagg's. Oh God, it's ghastly. To see him there. I . . . I can hardly believe it."

"That's three." Daphne's voice was a whisper. "Three dead." Then she started to sob.

Mary wanted to comfort her but felt as if she herself might faint. The room kept blurring, fading, dissolving into a multi-coloured mist and the thought uppermost in her mind was how unpleasant was sugared tea. She must show self-control. She must. She didn't want Denis to see her being weak and silly. She forced herself to speak. "Are you sure he's dead?"

Denis said wearily. "Absolutely. Someone used the mallet he breaks up hard clay with. It was lying there beside him. I picked it up. It was all . . . blood and hair and . . . There's nothing we can do for him. Nothing at all." He looked across at Daphne. "Pull yourself together, Daphne. It's been a terrible shock but we mustn't go to pieces. The first step is to notify the authorities."

"Oh yes," said Mary. "We must phone the police."

"Why phone them when they're already here? We'll tell one of the constables. They *are* the police." Denis spoke spiritlessly, staring at the wall. His tone was wooden as he went on. "The back constable wasn't there. He isn't always. And Tom was at his kiln.

So I went through into his studio and . . . there he was. On the floor. And the mallet . . . "

"Oh, Denis."

He tossed his head, as if trying to shake off a condition of stupor, then spoke again with an obvious effort at control. "I'm sorry, girls. I'm sorry I've had to tell you this. But it's happened and we must try to be calm about it." He looked suddenly angry, setting his lips and thrusting forth his chin. "Some swine, someone here in the house at this very minute, must've done it."

Mary asked, "Denis, was he . . . could you tell . . . has he been dead long?"

He turned to her. "How can I tell? About half an hour? Some time anyway. The blood on his head was all congealed and darkening. Oh, sorry. But you did ask. Look, somebody did it. Somebody in the house probably the same person who killed Clagg and Josie. No outsider came through the front door while we were here. And no one could get round the back without being seen by the constable at the gate. Therefore, you see? Before we inform the police I think we should check up on the whereabouts of everyone else, do you agree? Oh, are you all right, Daphne? You've lost all your colour."

"I'm okay. I'm not going to faint like last time. But oh . . . it's terrible."

"Yes," said Denis grimly. "It *is* terrible and someone in the building right now is responsible."

"At least Mary and I were together all the time," said Daphne.

"Unfortunately that will be no alibi. It was done before any of us were in this room, by the look of him. We'll all be suspected. There'll be hell to pay. More questioning and no kid gloves this time. That's why I suggest it would be sensible to check up on the others. Daphne, do you feel fit enough to go upstairs and see if Hugh's in his room? I'll go to the Martins and you, Mary, if you don't mind, to Mrs Dibbett."

"Mrs Dibbett wouldn't have done it, poor old dear."

"All the same, we must include her. It may be of advantage later if we can confirm that she was in her room when we checked and say what she was doing. Don't tell them there's anything wrong, though. Are you both fit to do it? Do you want more tea first? I could go round them all if you prefer but it would save time if you helped."

"We'll go," said Mary. "And that tea didn't help. It was foul. Let's go."

"Remember, it's important not to look upset. Just call in to ask some trivial question, anything that occurs to you at the time. But take notice whether any of *them* are upset. Breathless, or disturbed in any way. Or even . . . blood on their clothes. They'll have had time to change but they may not have had the opportunity, or may not have thought it necessary. Get them to turn round, if you can. Point to something out the window, perhaps, and then look at the back of their clothes, where they might not suspect any stain to be. We'll

151

meet back here. Are you sure you're all right, Daphne?"

"Yes," Daphne assured him. "I can do it. It's just that it's been such an awful shock."

"Of course it has. You look so pale. Here, put your head down. Like that . . . right down. There. Stay like that a minute. Better?" Denis was looking at her with concern but Mary noticed that he, too, was pale. Poor Denis, to have been the one to find Tom there. One thought of Denis as a rock, unshakeable, steady and firm. It was rather nice to see that he was human.

Daphne got to her feet in a few moments and Denis said, "Right. You know where to go. Make any excuse you like for calling. Don't hurry. Don't look upset. Take it easy, so they don't suspect. You go up the stairs first, Daphne. I'll follow in a second or two."

They were soon back in Mary's flat comparing results. Mrs Dibbett had been sewing up the seams of a baby's matinee jacket, the Martins watching television and Hugh writing a letter to the editor of the *Herald*. And all four of them had looked upset.

"So that wasn't much use," said Daphne.

"Yes, it was," Denis told her. "We know where they were shortly after Tom was found and that may be of help to the police. Now we must get our own story straight. We have nothing to hide but when you're under shock, it's easy to become confused and state facts which are wrong. They'll ask me when I found him. When I left the room it was eleven o'clock. The St Andrew's church bells were just starting up, remember, to announce the beginning of morning service? so that would be eleven. What's the time by you now? I make it twelve minutes past. Good heavens, we'll be ticked off for taking so long to notify the police."

"Is that all it's been?" sighed Daphne. "It seems ages." She sank onto a chair and let her hands hang limply by her sides.

"It's far too long. "Twelve minutes! They'll go mad. I'll phone them right away. But I still think we were wise to check on where the others were. Did you look carefully for any blood stains? I didn't see any on the Martins but they were sitting down and I couldn't think of any way to make them stand up."

The girls shook their heads. Mary said, "I thought you were going to tell the constable instead of phoning?"

"Yes, but we've delayed so long. He'd have to come inside to phone so it'll be quicker if I do it myself. And I found the poor guy, so I guess it's my responsibility. Where's your phone book, Mary? I say, are you all right? As soon as I've phoned I'm going to make you two a strong cup of coffee. I could do with some myself too. We'll have to answer questions." He brushed one hand across his forehead but it did not erase the worried frown. He picked up the phone book and his hands shook as he fumbled with the pages. "We don't want 111 in this case, do we? No, I'll ring Central and ask for Operations. I think that's the procedure. Where the hell is it? Here we are. *Police* . . . oh, *refer Government Departments*. Why the blazes can't they just put the number there as well? *Services numbers . . . STD codes . . . Registered Medical Practitioners* . . . where the bloody . . . oh, here it is. He dialled. "Operations, please. Oh, I'm sorry. I was trying to get the police." He replaced the receiver. "Damn and blast. I can't even dial straight." He tried again, slowly and carefully. "Police? Operations, please . . . I am phoning from Fairway Flats, Symonds Street. I have to report a death . . . "

It was the first time Mary had ever heard him swear.

8

"ONE of your parishioners resides in the building and is doubtless suffering from shock. It must be a terrible experience for a woman of her age."

The reverend Jabal Jarrett smiled. "And you want me to believe that you've come to see me this morning in order to remind me of my obligations — *comfort all that mourn* — *bind up the broken-hearted*?"

"I don't pretend any such thing," said Inspector Chambers. "I have a higher regard for your perspicuity. I merely mention the old lady's plight as an additional possible incentive. You know damned well why I've come."

"To be converted to the Christian faith? A pleasure. Any time."

"Cut it out, Jabe."

"Trevor, I am not . . . "

"Now don't start that," growled the inspector. "I know what you're going to say. I can say it for you. You are not trained, I admit, as I and my men are, in the skills of checking, tracing, analysing. You don't have our resources for research, the use of forensic labs and extensive manpower. You don't have the same access to records and private documents. True."

"Then why the . . . ?"

"You know why. You've helped us on several previous occasions. You have gifts which we don't have time to develop. You seem to be able to get inside a criminal mind and understand how it works."

"No one knows another's mind."

"Not entirely but you have a certain understanding of the anti-social, and the ability to identify them. Perhaps because you have contact with so many different personalities, whereas we see mainly the lawbreakers, the accused, the suspected. They're not always guilty. We interview numerous persons innocent of the crime we're investigating, but at the time they're usually under stress, frightened, nervous, not themselves, and often trying to conceal some trivial secret in their private life which has nothing to do with the crime, wouldn't interest us and clouds the issue. You meet all types, in normal as well as traumatic circumstances, and that helps you distinguish the devil from the saint."

"Neither of which exists. We're all a mixture of both."

"But the mixture varies in its proportions. You've maintained at times that in any group of suspects there's always one who shows himself most likely to be the guilty person. You've frequently sorted him out for us. You can sniff out evil. And God knows, there's enough of it around these days."

"*The wicked walk on every side*?" suggested Jabal.

"If you *must* put it that way. Do the wicked walk on every side in your parish?"

"They're a typical cross-section of Aucklanders. Some fine folk among them, and a few of the other sort."

The inspector leaned forward and wagged a finger. "And that's exactly what I'm getting at, my boy. You meet all types in a wide variety of circumstances, whereas the types I deal with, the type round the city in these evil times . . ."

"What do you mean, 'evil times'. They're no worse than they used to be. St Paul described a section of the populace in his day as *being filled with all unrighteousness, fornication, wickedness, covetousness, maliciousness, full of envy, murder, debate, deceit, malignity, whispers . . .*"

"Are you making that up as you go?"

"Not at all. I could continued, *backbiters, haters of God, despiteful, without understanding covenant breakers, without natural affection, implacable, unmerciful . . .* All right, I can't remember the rest of it. But

159

I assure you he covered the field. Observant chap, Paul. So you see people have not changed since his day. They're no worse now. I like those I meet in my work. I admire many of them greatly and know they're better men than I."

"And the others?"

"Well . . . they have their lapses — don't we all? But most of them mean well. Nearly all men and women have a sincere wish to be good, if they don't get hurt in the process."

"I didn't mean to insult your flock. Perhaps it's because so many of them are worthy types that you've developed this ability to detect a criminal among them. Now stop trying to needle me with quotations or I'll retaliate with a few clauses from the Crimes Act. And you won't distract me from my purpose in coming to see you. You know why I'm here. I want your help."

"You don't need the help of a suburban vicar and I haven't the time to give it, even if I thought myself capable of doing so."

"Jabal, we ask the help of all sorts. We're not too proud to employ hypnotists, self-styled seers, gurus, tarot card readers. We're ready to listen to a nut who phones up and tells us he's dreamed where a body is hidden or what weapon was used. We can't afford to ignore any possible lead. The press loves to get hold of something like that and blow it up. *Police consult fortune-teller* and so on. What they don't realise is that we're not bowing to superstition or E.S.P. The teacup reader or the vision sighter may unconsciously be recalling something heard or seen, something essential to the case, and imagine he's had a psychic experience. So we play along with his own account of how he learned the facts. All we know is that something triggered off his memory and what he tells us may be of use. Anyway, you're not in that category. You arrive at your conclusions through logical deduction and knowledge of humanity. Oh, come on, Jabe. You've helped before."

"On each occasion when you've involved me I've been on holiday or had time to spare. I haven't now."

"Why not? Whatever do you *do* all day? No, don't answer that. I couldn't stand any more Bible quotes." Trevor Chambers looked keenly at his friend, hoping that his interest was being aroused. He knew what usually did it — the enticement of a problem, a challenge, combined with an appeal to his compassion for all those who suffered, the guilty as well as the innocent, and the need to prevent further tragedy. Those were the ingredients of the bait he used. But it was taking longer than usual to hook his victim.

Jabal was frowning, looking out his study window, so at least he must be considering it. Trevor waited nearly a full minute, then said quietly, "I'll just run over the facts again." The vicar voiced no objection and Trevor began, "You know about Clagg. I could've sworn that was an outside job. The subsequent murders throw doubt on it, but there's still not a vestige of a motive other than robbery. Nothing in his effects to indicate an enemy. The post-mortem confirmed death from the knife wound."

"Wasn't that obvious?"

We always have an autopsy. He could've had a heart attack before he was stabbed, or have taken poison. It has to be checked."

"I gather no one was seen hanging round the house, or going in?"

"Oh, yes indeed. The public have been most co-operative."

"What? You have a description of the intruder?"

"A very full one, from seven eye witnesses. He was a tall thin young man of late middle age, shorter than average and thickset, with curly brown hair on his bald scalp, clean-shaven, with a dark beard and sideburns. He was dressed in blue jeans of a dark green colour, wore a short-sleeved open shirt with one cuff torn at the wrist, and a blue-patterned tie . . . need I go on?"

"I see."

"To put it in other words, we've got nowhere. So much for Clagg. The woman Wallace was poisoned. She collapsed while drinking coffee and we think that was the medium used. The poison seems to have been a rapid acting type but has not yet been identified. The boys are still working on it. Unfortunately the woman appears to have rinsed her mug before succumbing. It was turned upside down on her sink bench — identified by other tenants as the one she used. We're hoping some trace remains in it or in the liquid retrieved from the sink. That would indicate that the poison was administered in the coffee and it will eventually be identified from examination of her blood and stomach contents."

"How long will that take?"

"Unless the forensic chaps know what

to look for, it can take weeks. An analysis is far from simple. It's more a case of think of a poison, then test for it. All rooms on the property and the garages were searched. Samples were taken of any possible lethal substances, even prescribed medicaments. The potter's rooms were full of poisons but we also found chemicals of some sort in every flat." He took a sheet of paper from his pocket. "Here we are. I brought you a list. The Martins had ergotamine tartrate and ferous fumerate. Hugh Fuller marijuana and stelazine, Denis Day dilante, Daphne de Vere, as she calls herself, had benzoyl peroxide and aspirin, Mary Grayson aspirin and cetrimide, and your old lady aspirin, cetylpyridium chloride and quinine sulphate. Mostly in chemists' mixture of doctors' prescriptions, or remedies bought off a chemist's shelf. But keep the list. You might get something from it."

Jabal took the sheet of paper and stared at it. "I've never heard of most of them. Could the poison have been swallowed earlier and taken effect when the woman drank the coffee?"

"You mean in capsule form? That's been considered. But a soft capsule would dissolve very rapidly in the hot coffee, which means the poison would have to be almost tasteless. The stomach juices would dissolve a harder coating, but the pathologist says there was no trace of a coating in the stomach contents. His opinion is that the poison was pure and was administered in the drink she took in Grayson's flat."

"Why didn't your poisoner use arsenic? It's quick, certain, and easy to get hold of."

"How the hell do I know? He could've had another poison readily available. The potter Solley probably had a rapid acting one among his materials and didn't need to go out buying arsenic, and he's the one with the best opportunity of administering the stuff. We also know that Solley was left-handed and the knife wound in Clagg showed a slight slope to the right. We were actually rustling up enough evidence to arrest him when he got himself killed, which more or less establishes his innocence. It's crazy, Jabal."

"You think one person responsible for all three deaths?"

"Not necessarily. But it's most likely, isn't it?"

"I suppose so. Coincidences do occur but seldom in threes like this."

"Yet there are three different methods used," said Trevor. "Knifing, poison and smashing a skull. Those who murder more than once tend to stick to one method, the tried and true. As for poison, most poisoners don't stop, can't stop. It becomes an obsession, gives them a thrill of enjoyment. Take William Palmer, Mary Ann Cotton, Thomas Neill Cream. So why was only one of these three poisoned?"

"You feel the killer is not running true to type?"

"Yes, and that indicates a certain

kind of personality, perhaps unusual intelligence or a rebel mind. That's where you can help, Jabe. Sort him out for us. Actually we have very little to do with premeditated murder. We're not as experienced in it as you might think because nearly all the cases of homicide we deal with are results of a fit of rage, usually under the influence of drugs or alcohol. Domestic quarrels, gang fights, brawls at a pub. Planned murder is far more difficult to investigate. My chief worry is that if some lunatic in these flats has killed three times, he can kill again."

"Yes," agreed Jabal. "Murder becomes progressively easier and also more tempting."

"We have men on the premises all day and night now, and C.I.B. chaps calling frequently. There's a big team in every murder enquiry — officer in charge of the body, officer in charge of the scene, officer in charge of effects, and each with assisting staff. It would be a bold killer who'd strike again with all of them buzzing in and out. And the tenants will be jolly careful. They're probably — all except one — huddling behind locked doors when they're not out at work. Yet we can't be *sure* of their safety. Poor wretches, they must be scared out of their wits."

"The killer is probably scared too," said Jabal. "That's the danger. He could strike again if he sees a risk to himself or even if a suspicion is voiced. Four murders bring no greater penalty than three."

"We did consider closing up the building and housing the inmates elsewhere. Decided against it. It's useful having them on the premises. In fact now we've finished with Clagg's flat, we've granted permission to the executors of the will, Dan, Corrie and Marsh, to let it again, and they've put it in the hands of an agent. I can't imagine anyone in his right mind wanting to move in but the rental accommodation is so desperate you never know. And a newcomer should be safe."

Jabal said, "Poison is usually a woman's weapon, isn't it? Could a woman have killed Solley? Delivered a blow strong enough?"

"The police surgeon thought it unlikely but possible and the pathologist agreed. A mallet was used and left beside the body, smothered with prints, including those of Day, who discovered the body. He says he picked it up. His are the only clear ones. There's such a conglomeration of others it's not much help. But the boys are working on it. We'd already taken prints of everyone in the house. Why do you ask if a woman could have struck the blow that killed Solley? Are you thinking of your old lady?"

"I can't imagine her bringing a mallet down on someone's head. But I don't entirely trust her. Her conversation is a mixture of shrewd remarks and concise, lucid statements, spattered with deliberately inconsequential chatter. She had a good education, she shows no signs of mental senility and at committee meetings she speaks succinctly and to the point. Last time I talked with her at the flats I felt she was putting on an act."

"You imagine she could've hired a hit man? In disapproval of potters, landlords and prostitutes?"

"No. Actually she liked Miss Wallace, or professed to, and she spoke well of the potter. And how could she find anyone to do the job? She's unlikely to have contacts in the right circles."

Trevor said, "Clagg's murder really looked like the work of vandals, after money or drugs and having a taste for destruction. Wallace? It's possible one of her clients could've had it in for her, but how could they do it? It's almost certain she drank the poison in that cup of coffee. As for Solley, it's difficult to see how anyone but one of the residents could've attacked him. The front door was locked. There was no constable at the back of the house at the time and if the one in front was looking the other way someone *could* have got over the fence and round the back. But what a hell of a risk! He'd have been seen coming out again, if not going in."

"How long had Solley been dead when he was found?"

"The chap who discovered him thought about twenty minutes to half an hour, but that's a layman's guess. The police surgeon said about half an hour from the time he examined him and that's only a rough estimate. There are so many factors to be taken into account — temperature of the room, stage of digestion, physical exertion. But half an hour would bring the time of the murder into the period when the back constable was away, as I said. Solley's back door was open, because although he was at his wheel, the furnace was going and he had a load in the kiln. So he'd be keeping an eye on it. Which all means that a stranger *could* have gone in that way. Unlikely but possible. He also had regular clients who used to go straight through his hall door. But they had first to be let into the house. No one admits to opening the door to a stranger and they would surely be glad to do so, to clear themselves of suspicion. In fact, it's surprising that no one has bothered to invent a stranger calling."

"So your murderer isn't very bright?"

"Or is over-confident. Any one of the tenants could've gone through Solley's flat and struck him while he was preoccupied at the wheel. A matter of minutes. Some of them were in the girl Grayson's flat when Day went to find Solley but they had not been there long, so that gives them no alibi."

"What about the fellow who found the body?"

"We considered him, of course. Very convenient finding the body of someone you've just knocked off. But if Wallace was poisoned at the coffee gathering, which seems certain, I don't see how he could've administered the poison. He took a packet of biscuits round the room but she didn't take one and he didn't go near enough to her to interfere with her mug. That's pretty well agreed. We questioned each one as to movement of the others and there was very little discrepancy in their testimony. Solley appears to have been the only one with adequate opportunity and he would've been taking a hell of a risk at the time. As for Day, he was the one, it seems, who stuck up for Wallace. Didn't approve her choice of profession but was indignant about the treatment meted out to her. Live and let live. Claimed she had qualities that compensated. I interviewed the fellow myself and I could swear he was genuinely upset over her death."

"How are the other tenants taking it?"

"They seem stunned, understandably so. I imagine they're thoroughly frightened, wondering who's going to be next. There's a limited number left. The couple called Martin, Maud Smith, alias Daphne de Vere, Mary Grayson, Denis Day, Hugh Fuller and your friend Dibbett. *She* must be in a

174

tizzy, poor old thing."

Jabal ignored this calculated reminder of his duties. "Are they just going to stay there, waiting to be killed?"

"I told you, our men are there, and it's easier to wind up the case if we've got the suspects on the premises. They're free to leave if they wish. We're not stopping them. So what about it, Jabe? You could at least talk with them."

"On what pretext? Pretend I've dropped by to save a soul or two? Or invite them to contribute to our Mission Fund?"

"I could tell them you're working with the Police and request them to answer any questions you may ask. Now come on, Jabal. I know you're busy but it won't hurt your curate to do a little extra. It's not just a matter of apprehending a murderer. It's one of preventing further deaths. Would you care to see Solley's premises? I can arrange that."

Jabal shook his head. "It wouldn't

help. As you said, I'm not trained in that type of detection. The scene would mean little to me. And I *have* seen his rooms. I met him. He showed me his kiln and wheel."

"How? When? You didn't tell me."

"*I went down to the potter's house and behold he wrought a work on the wheel.* Oh, sorry. It's habit. It was when I went to see Mrs Dibbett and actually he wasn't at the wheel. He was firing."

"And what did you think of him?"

"Rough, enthusiastic, short-tempered. I couldn't judge a man in that short time and I wasn't regarding him as a future murderer. Well, I don't want any further killings, Trevor any more than you do. I don't know that I can help. I certainly can't promise to find your killer. But I'm willing to go and talk to the tenants."

"Good. Wear your collar. The killer might be afraid of hell fire and confess when he sees it."

"I don't preach hell fire, you heathen."

9

IT was not until the evening that Jabal found time to visit Fairway Flats. After some consideration, he had put on his clerical collar.

He parked his car outside the Old Choral Hall and walked down to the flats. It was nearing seven o'clock. Symonds Street at this hour has lost its bustling daytime activity. Workers have made their way home from the city, buses are infrequent, traffic is thin. In September the street lights are not yet switched on, the sun has disappeared behind the downtown high rise blocks, and a dull uniform greyness shows up the irregular shape of the old buildings and the contrasting lines of the new. In the sullen atmosphere one can hear a continuous low rumbling from the distant wharves and railway yards.

It is now that emerge the creatures of the night. They crawl out from their hideaways, from the narrow side streets, from sheds, hovels, and the concealing bushes of the old Grafton cemetery — a sorry medley of alcoholics, prostitutes, perverts, muggers, gang members, sneak thieves and the pathetic, foul-smelling glue-sniffing 'street kids', wandering, prowling, searching, forming into threes, fours, sixes, looking for easy victims to rob, for an unlocked car to drive, or simply for another hole to huddle in while they smoke their pot.

The prudent man does not walk alone at dusk in lower Symonds Street and clerical garb is no passport to safety. But Jabal felt more pity than fear as he passed by the muttering, shuffling groups.

One light showed in the upper storey of Fairway Flats. The rest of the house was unlit and the dusty twilight emphasised the dingy dilapidated state of its exterior. Above the rickety picket fence now rose a land agent's sign, *Flat to Let. Apply . . .* But the *Flat* had been crossed through in thick black crayon and another word substituted. The sign now read *Coffin to Let*. Had it been amended by some embittered tenant to put off prospective applicants? Or by a resentful neighbour? Or by the murderer, challenging the police and the public to try to stop him, warning them in advance to expect a further victim? Jabal hoped it was rather the work of some facetious passing student, in a childish bid to catch the public eye with a display of his wit. *Everyone that passeth by shall be astonished and wag his head.*

It didn't matter who had done it. It must go. With not even a fleeting thought of the eighth commandment Jabal tugged angrily at the board and after a few minutes managed to pull the supporting stake out of the ground. He carried board and stake back to his car and stowed them in the boot. The agent would be able to let the flat without the sign. He would already have received phone calls, in spite of the publicity given to the murders. Desperate flat hunters would not all be deterred by the deaths of a few people they didn't even know.

He rang the bell and shortly the door opened two inches. It was now on a chain. "Who is it?" asked a young voice and one eye looked at him.

"My name is Jarrett. I . . . "

But his clerical collar had been glimpsed and the door was opened before he need explain further. A young woman stood looking at him, her face so white and anxious that instead of introducing himself fully and explaining his errand, he asked, "Are you all right?"

"Oh, yes, thank you," she said. "I think so. I just . . . I didn't know who it was. We never do. There've been . . . that is . . . Did you come about the flat to let? You have to go to the agent. There's no one here to let it and we can't show you over."

"No, I didn't come about the flat."

He was tempted to add a warning about opening the door to a stranger simply because he wore his collar back to front. But he had no time before she spoke again.

"Oh, did you see that awful notice outside? Is that what you've come about? It *is* horrible but we don't know who did it. I didn't."

Another reaction to his collar. Assuming, as many laymen did, that the clergy are guardians of public morals who spend their time reproving what they consider wrong. "I've removed it," he told her, "although I had no right to interfere with an agent's signboard. It was a crude reference to the tragedies that have occurred here."

"I didn't do it and Mrs Dibbett wouldn't and not the Martins. They don't do anything like that." There was a hint of criticism in her tone. "And Denis is far too sensible. I think it must have been Hugh or Daphne. They protest, you see. Oh, I'm sorry. You don't even know who

I'm talking about, do you? They're the other tenants here." She drew a hand across her forehead.

Jabal said, "My name is Jarrett. I'm the vicar of St Bernard's and one of the tenants here, Mrs Dibbett, attends our church. I called in the hopes of seeing her. I thought she may be very upset at the recent events and would like an opportunity to move into temporary accommodation elsewhere."

"Oh, come in, then. I'm Mary Grayson and that's my flat, number two. Poor Mrs Dibbett, yes. I bet she *is* upset. How could she help it at her age? It must be worse for her than any of us, although she tries not to show it. She's awfully brave. That's her door and I think she's in."

Jabal paused in the hall and looked with concern at her pallid, drawn countenance. "Miss Grayson, are you frightened?"

She opened wide hazel eyes. "There've been three murders here. Of course I'm frightened. Scared stiff. We're all looking for somewhere else to go. The police are here and they put this chain on the door for us which was decent of them but they wouldn't've done it if they really thought we were safe, would they? So we want to get away out of it but you know what it's like now trying to find a flat or even a room. Can you really find temporary accommodation, like you said? For anyone, I mean? Or just your church people?"

"It must be very distressing for you all."

"The married couple upstairs are desperate. They're going to have a baby. Could you . . . sort of take our names just in case?"

"Certainly. I can understand your desire to shift and I may be able to arrange something. But haven't the police offered you alternative accommodation?"

"Well, not offered it exactly. More sort of threatened it. They said they might move us all out and close up the building. It sounded as if they'd stow us in cells or detention centres."

Jabal smiled. "No, they have other resources. But I'll see what I can do. Suppose I come over to your flat when I've had a word with Mrs Dibbett? Will you be in?"

"Yes. We're scared to go out now, even in pairs. Though we're probably safer when we *are* out, don't you reckon?"

"You have nothing to fear now. The police have the house under constant surveillance." He hoped he was speaking the truth. "I'll see you shortly."

Mary went back to her flat and Jabal knocked on Mrs Dibbett's door.

Mrs Dibbett gave every appearance of being herself grieved and anxious. Her hair was for once out of place and even her dress not as neat as usual. Her wrinkled face was set in a worried frown, which cleared a little when she saw who her visitor was. "Oh, vicar, come in. How nice to see you. Is it because I didn't come to church last Sunday? I wasn't ill exactly but there have been some terrible things going on here. Have you heard? It's all been in the papers. Do sit down, vicar. That poor girl, Josie."

"Yes. A dreadful tragedy."

"She didn't deserve to be killed. Josie was a kind person. Oh, I know what she did was wrong, but she never hurt anyone. And she's dead — *dead*. Someone killed her. Poisoned her. It's terrible. And poor Mr Solley too. Both dead."

"And Mr Clagg," added Jabal.

"Oh *him*!" She waved that away. "The world is better without him. But not Josie. And Mr Solley was such a clever potter. Why *shouldn't* he have a beard? Really, I didn't feel like coming to church. I hope you don't mind."

"Of course I don't mind, Mrs Dibbett. You attend church at your own free will. There is no obligation to do so. I didn't call on that account. Do you know yet what the future of these flats is?"

"No. The inspector — such a nice man he is, vicar — he told us that Mr Clagg left a will, naming a relative in England. A firm of solicitors in Auckland are the executors and they're handling his affairs now until probate — is that what you call it? — anyway, until the new owner takes over. I suppose he'll sell it, since he lives in England. So where will we go then? Poor Mrs Martin."

"Probate may not be granted for some time, Mrs Dibbett. You'll probably be left here meantime but do you want to stay in a house where such tragedies have occurred?"

"It's very convenient here."

"You're not afraid to stay?"

"Afraid of what, vicar? Oh, you mean being put out on the street? Yes, that could happen and it would be most awkward. I hope you're right about probate taking some time. I could go down to one of my sons if the worst came to the worst, but I'd much rather not."

Jabal suspected that she had deliberately pretended to misunderstand him. Yet she didn't look afraid for herself. He said on an impulse, "Have you any idea who committed the three murders here?"

"Why, how should I know, vicar? I don't think it was Mrs Martin — that's the lady upstairs, the one who's going to have a baby, and *he* wouldn't, even if he wanted to. And it wouldn't be Mary or Daphne. Of course you haven't met them, have you? But they really wouldn't, I'm sure. It must've been someone who just wandered in off the street."

"On three separate occasions? I don't think you really believe that."

She looked at him without speaking, the picture of guileless, pathetic old age.

He spoke sternly. "Mrs Dibbett, if you know anything at all about these killings, it is your duty to inform the police."

"Oh, I would, vicar, I would. Now

will you have a cup of tea?"

"No thank you." He tried again. "If you have a suspicion, if you saw anyone acting strangely, if you heard a remark passed that made you wonder, if you know of some unusual happening, however trivial, that might possibly have some connection . . . "

She was hardly listening. She broke in, "Oh, of course, Mr Jarrett. I would certainly tell the police. Such nice, polite men. Quite courteous and *so* understanding." The blue eyes looked at him with studied innocence.

He realised he was getting nowhere. If she knew anything at all she was not going to tell him. Whether through obstinacy or genuine ignorance, she was not going to talk. He knew when he was beaten and rose to his feet. "If you think of anything which might help you'll let the police know? Or contact me if you prefer."

"Oh, I shall, vicar, of course. And I'll be at church next Sunday. Hasn't Mrs Powell mended the altar hangings well? I hope you noticed. So clever with a needle."

He let her shut the door behind him before he walked across to knock on that of Mary Grayson. As Mary ushered him in a man rose courteously from the shabby couch. "This is Denis Day," said Mary. "He has a room upstairs. Denis came down to see how I was and I told him what you said about other accommodation. Then we got Mr Martin because it's so urgent for him and his wife."

Another man got belatedly to his feet. He was rabbity-faced with receding chin, a spotty skin and a frightened expression. Jabal was introduced and noted that Mary correctly remembered both his name and that of his church. He shook hands with both men, assessing each for his murdering potential. Denis Day's grip was firm and he looked mature and sensible, not the type one would expect to find in a third-rate Symonds Street bed-sitting room, but in this time of housing shortage one took what one could get. Mr Martin's hand was limp and moist. He gave the impression that he was incapable of any decisive action. So three years ago, had appeared the vicious killer of two teenage shop assistants.

"Please sit down, Mr Jarrett," said Mary, and Jabal noticed that although Martin had already flopped back into his chair, Denis Day waited until Jabal had sat before he did so himself. Good manners were rare now, and welcome, but had little to do with one's propensity to annihilate a neighbour or two.

Martin said, "Can you get us a flat? My wife's going to have a baby. If they sell this place we won't have anywhere to go and it's a dreadful place to be living in now."

"I didn't say Mr Jarrett had any flats up his sleeve," said Mary. "He just offered to take our names in case something turned up."

"It's a terrible situation for us,"

moaned Martin. "It shouldn't be allowed."

Jabal turned to Denis Day. "And are you interested in temporary quarters, Mr Day, until you find somewhere suitable?"

Denis hesitated, then said, "I don't think so. Not unless we're served notice to quit. It's far from pleasant to be residing in a place where there have been three murders, but it's a handy position for me. I work at the University. Of course if the place is sold and we're given notice, I'll have to start hunting. In the meantime, I think we men should be able to defend ourselves. But I want Mary to move out of all possible danger. I've been trying to persuade her for the last few days, so your offer is most opportune."

"I don't want to go unless we *all* go," said Mary. She *did* want to go. She desperately wanted to get right away from the place. But she couldn't leave Hugh, she simply couldn't bear it. She mustn't leave unless Hugh, too, was shifting out.

"You must, Mary." Denis was looking at her anxiously. "We can't risk anything happening to you." There was a slight emphasis on the 'you'. "Mary works at the Farmers', Mr Jarrett, and what worries me most is her coming home after nine o'clock on late shopping night."

"I often get a lift."

"Not always. And I don't always know what bus you'll be on, or else I'd meet you. Can you really arrange something, Mr Jarrett?"

"Within a few days, I should think. There are frequent demands on the emergency housing centres, mostly from battered wives, but there are other possibilities. Some of my parishioners could be approached. I'm sure one would be willing to put you up for a few weeks, Miss Grayson, while you hunt for something permanent. Of course, our district is further from your work."

Mary said nothing. If Hugh moved there would be no point in staying. She'd want to get out as soon as she could. It *was* so scary now, and it was decent of the vicar to offer his help. But Hugh didn't seem at all frightened and didn't speak of moving.

"And what about me and my wife?" asked Martin. "We can't stay here."

"It must be most unpleasant for you all," agreed Jabal.

"Oh, it's awful," said Mary. "There are police all over the place and they're not nice any more. Not friendly, as they were. They look sort of angry and they fire questions at us suddenly and don't seem to believe anything we say. They're horrid, aren't they, Den?"

"I don't find them so, Mary. They're just doing their job as best they can. They weren't particularly polite to me but I can't really blame them. I found Tom Solley's body, Mr Jarrett, and it was twelve minutes before I notified the police. They were most annoyed at that."

"You should have phoned the police straight away," said Cecil Martin. "That's the thing to do. You dial 111."

"We wanted to see where everyone in the house was. It seemed a good idea at the time but the police don't think so. Oh, it didn't take more than five or six minutes to check up but — well, I'd been in here with Mary and Daphne — that's another tenant, a young girl — and had to bring them back the news. They were naturally extremely upset. We all were. I thought Daphne was going to faint at one stage. It took us some time to compose ourselves."

"And then Denis dialled the wrong number," went on Mary, "and we talked and — well, the time just went. You wouldn't think they'd be so mad at just twelve minutes' delay. He was dead. We couldn't help him."

"How do you know it was twelve minutes?"

"It seemed more like an hour," said Mary. "It was awful. We just sort of sat there at first and couldn't take it in, Daphne and me. But Denis had heard the church bells start up and so he knew the time when he went out to look for Tom. We were going to ask him to come and have a cup of tea with us. Oh, poor Tom." She bit her lip, paused, then went on with an effort. "And before Denis rang the police we checked the time. We all have digital watches and it was exactly twelve minutes past eleven. And we thought the police would be pleased to know but they weren't. They were beastly about it, especially to Denis."

"They were justified," admitted Denis. "I see that now. It was no help to check the time when I phoned, as all calls are recorded with the time received. I should've remembered that. When a crisis occurs one doesn't always behave as one would like to. It was a terrible shock to find Tom killed and it really knocked me. Knocked some of the sense out of me, I'm afraid. I tried to act calmly and to look after the girls but all the time my head was reeling. I can't expect the police to understand. They're used to seeing the result of physical violence — broken limbs, gunshot wounds, smashed skulls and the like."

"Everyone knows to dial 111," said Martin.

Mary shot him a hostile glance. "I think Denis was very sensible the way he handled it. You didn't lose your head, Den, like Daphne and me. I don't know what we'd have done if you hadn't been there. Suppose one of *us* had gone in and found him!" she shuddered. "I think I'd have just stood there and screamed." She turned to Martin. "And I bet you would've too."

Cecil opened his mouth to protest but had not yet found the words when Jabal asked, "Have you any theory as to the reason for these dreadful murders, Mr Martin? Or as to who committed them?"

"I couldn't say," said Martin. "Vera

and I know nothing about it and we're not used to being mixed up in such a business. We oughtn't to be here. It's not right."

"Mr Day?"

Denis was looking at Cecil Martin with some amusement. He said, "We have some odd types here. One female punk but she's no killer. One anti-establishment young man with strange ideas and unpredictable behaviour, but I'm sure he couldn't kill either."

"Hugh's not like that, if you mean him," broke in Mary indignantly. "He's not 'strange'. He simply believes in justice for all and in social reform. He's very sincere, Mr Jarrett, and he gets awfully depressed at times because of the way things are. He wants to help everyone. He wouldn't kill."

"Of course he wouldn't," agreed Denis. "And he *is* sincere. He certainly has some influence over you, to persuade you to join in his weird activities. You're not really in tune with them."

197

"They are *not* weird. There's always some good purpose to them and I *like* to join in. Why shouldn't I? *I'm* not too stuffy to take part. We're having a march down Queen Street next Saturday, Mr Jarrett, against the Springbok tour. Anti-apartheid."

Denis laughed. "Actually, it's *pro* the tour, according to Hugh."

"Oh well, it's the same thing. He's willing to stand up for whatever he thinks is right. Freedom for our footballers to play whoever they want to. Mix with anyone. That *is* anti-apartheid, isn't it, Mr Jarrett?"

Denis said quickly, "Mary, we mustn't waste Mr Jarrett's time. We're all unusual in our way and I didn't mean to criticise Hugh. He's just a rebel, that's all. Daphne's a bit strange too but she's very young and she'll grow out of it. Solley himself was an oddity."

"A most peculiar man," agreed Martin.

"In what way?" asked Jabal.

"He was a typical artist," said Cecil. "Full of himself, always trying to get attention. Have you seen his notice? 'solley's pots'? He wouldn't use capitals. A very silly man."

"He was far from silly." objected Denis. "Just unusual. He made a few mugs and vases asymmetrical on purpose. It's amazing, but they sold as quickly as the others. There are plenty of people willing to be convinced that what is ugly is original and what is original is good. They equate 'different' with 'desirable'. So Solley's misshapen, deformed pottery sold well."

"There was something very fishy about him," persisted Cecil. "Two years ago he suddenly grew a beard."

"Why shouldn't he?" demanded Mary. "And beards don't grow 'suddenly'. Lots of men have beards so that doesn't make him fishy, *does* it, Den?"

"It depends why he grew it. Why does a man grow a beard, Mr Jarrett?"

"Not necessarily from evil motives," said Jabal. "A young man may want to look older, an older one may favour a patriarchal image and a man of any age may wish to hide a weak chin or a skin rash or a profile he considers unattractive to women. It could simply be an effort to add distinction to a nondescript face, or the result of adulation of a bearded hero. Solley was an artist and some famous old masters had beards. But the most common reason is sheer laziness, to avoid the necessity of daily shaving."

"That's a charitable view," said Denis. "A beard can also be grown to hide an identifying scar or birthmark, to prevent the police recognising the face as one on a Wanted list, or to prevent some past criminal accomplices from discovering the whereabouts of someone who double-crossed them. Solley had been in prison."

"The police will investigate his past history thoroughly," said Jabal. "But suppose someone came here for the purpose of killing him, could he have got into the house?"

"Yes, if he'd waited his chance. The constable at the back of the house was not there all day. They used him for messages and various jobs. Anyone could see him walk off and seize the opportunity to get in. It would need a bit of daring and a cool head but it could be done. And who could trace him once he'd walked out? He'd get clean away with it." Denis looked at Jabal, then smiled and shrugged his shoulders. "And you don't believe that theory any more than I do. Someone here killed poor old Tom. Someone in the house knifed Clagg, poisoned Josie and then murdered Solley. Have you seen that notice outside. *Coffin to let?* Whoever wrote that must be expecting, or even planning, another murder."

"I've seen it and removed it."

"Oh, don't talk about that," said Mary, anxious to change the subject. It could only have been Hugh who altered the sign. No one else would think of it. And why shouldn't he, if he wanted to? It was his way of making a comment to the world, lodging a protest. He wouldn't have realised how much it would upset them all. So she said, "Mr Jarrett, can you really find accommodation for everyone here? It's really urgent for Cecil and Vera. Gosh, they might have their baby any minute."

Jabal glanced across to Vera and said, "I doubt it. *The stork in the heaven knoweth her appointed time.*"

Denis gave a slight smile. "I haven't heard *that* quoted from the pulpit."

"Jeremiah. I admit his meaning was a little different. You attend church, then?"

"No, I don't. I haven't been since my parents dragged me there at six years of age."

"We none of us go to church," admitted Mary. "Except Hugh. He's been at times. He tries *everything* once. And Mrs Dibbett, of course."

"We used to go," Cecil Martin claimed. "We were regular church goers. It's just that with the baby coming and other . . . er . . . commitments . . . "

"I didn't come here to persuade any of you to attend church," said Jabal, "but to see whether you would welcome temporary accommodation elsewhere. Perhaps you would care to talk it over with the rest of the household? In the meantime I can make enquiries and find out what is available. Would it be convenient, Miss Grayson, if you all met me here in your flat one evening? I could then report on what is offering."

"Oh, would you really? That would be neat. Is Sunday evening possible? That would be best, wouldn't it, Denis? That's when everyone is usually home. I could round them all up, tell them you're coming."

"Sunday evening would do nicely," said Jabal. It would not do nicely. It would be very inconvenient. Any other evening would have suited him better. But he wanted to see as many of the tenants as possible. The curate could manage on his own. "You'll have

203

everyone here next Sunday? Including Mrs Dibbett?"

"Oh yes. She goes to bed early, though. So could you come at seven? Would that do?" Mary was looking at him eagerly. He noticed that she was no longer pale.

"Isn't Hugh going to a meeting of the Campaign Against Corporal Punishment?" Denis reminded her.

"No, it's the Bi-Lingual Promotion Society next Sunday and the Maori speaker couldn't come so they've put it off. Of course, he might have something else on by now. He's always doing something, Mr Jarrett. He doesn't stand around idle. Not Hugh." Her eyes were lit up and the soft tone in her voice was not lost on either Denis or the Vicar.

"He *sits* around idle," said Denis. "He'll mope for hours."

"That's only when he's thinking. He gets very depressed about the world today and he has to think up ways to protest. He says the trouble is that most people are too apathetic, too ready to sit back and let others look after their interests for them. But I'll try to have him here, Mr Jarrett. When he knows you're helping to find somewhere for everyone in the house, and you are, aren't you? Then he'll come, I'm sure he'll come. Won't he, Denis?" She was chattering with animation now.

"Of course he will, Mary, we'll see to it." The protective tone in his voice was noticeable and it was not too hard to guess that he wished Mary were equally anxious that he, too, should be present. "It's very good of you, Mr Jarrett, to take such trouble to help us. If you could just get lodging for the girls, it would be a weight off our minds."

"It's very urgent for my wife and me," whined Martin. "We must have somewhere to go. It's simply dreadful."

Jabal rose. "I'll do what I can. I must go now." The meeting of the Stewardship Committee would already have started without him.

10

JABAL, delayed by a caller, was the last to arrive on Sunday evening at Mary Grayson's flat. The best chair had been reserved for him. The seven tenants welcomed him politely, almost deferentially, and now they sat around Mary's living room, looking at him expectantly, waiting for him to solve their problems, as if, being a clergyman, he had special powers not bestowed on laymen. He felt ashamed of deceiving them as to his full motive for coming. He had certainly, as arranged, made enquiries and extracted offers of help from suitable parishioners. He would report this to them. But he also wanted to listen to them talk, talk not only of their accommodation worries, the deaths of their fellow tenants and the attitude of the police, but just talk — discuss the Budget, the riot at

Western Springs, the theft of parrots from the zoo, the latest Ranfurly shield match and the weather. For in their talk all men in time betray their character and Jabal hoped to identify, among these seven, a triple murderer.

Mary introduced to him those he had not met before. 'Vera Martin.' A small nervous woman with untidy hair and a long face, outwardly a colourless character like her husband and, like him, giving the impression of being incapable of decisive action. But more than one seemingly timid female has taken up a carving knife and vented years of suppressed emotion on her spouse, her lodger or her next-door neighbour.

'Hugh Fuller.' Here was the antithesis of the Martins. Here was vitality, intelligence, and possible lawlessness, a disregard for convention and perhaps for other peoples' lives.

'Daphne de Vere.' A young girl, Jabal was unaware that Daphne's neat dress tonight was entirely in his honour. Mary had used some persuasion. 'He's doing us a favour,' she had pointed out. 'He'll never get you a place if you come along dressed punk. It's not that there's anything wrong with it,' she had added hurriedly, 'but couldn't you — just for once? It's not being hypocritical. It's just polite and it's common sense as well. After all, you dress like anyone else during the week.' Daphne had given in and Mary thought how pretty she was. Without her grotesque make-up she also looked fragile and very young. She was only nineteen.

Mrs Dibbett was sitting primly, her hands folded demurely in her lap. Denis Day was in the chair beside her.

They had evidently had some discussion before Jabal came and agreed on questions to be asked and statements to be made. Hugh Fuller spoke first. He rose to his feet and stood by the old-fashioned, bricked up fireplace, one hand on the mantelpiece, one foot on the fender. It was a dramatic pose.

The young man was an exhibitionist. But so are many of his age and yet lead blameless lives. "Mr Jarrett, Mary asked you to help us and we're grateful if you're willing to do so. But some of us don't want to accept help under false pretences. Mary said you were going to ask the people who go to your church if they had a room to spare. So I want to tell you, right now, that Daphne and I couldn't accept that, because we don't go to church. We're all for freedom of the individual and that includes freedom from religion. We're *unbelievers*. I've been to church a few times, but only from curiosity to see what goes on." He looked defiantly at Jabal, his cheeks flushed, his eyes bright.

What did he expect? A shocked reaction? A refusal to help? An order to leave the room now hallowed by the presence of an insignificant, hard-working suburban vicar, whose last task before he came had been to accompany a member of the Mothers' Union over to the church hall, roll up his sleeves and unblock the kitchen sink?

Mary said, "Oh, does it matter? None of us go to church except Mrs Dibbett."

Vera Martin whined, "It's just we're so tired on Sunday, you see, reverend. It's not that we don't want to . . ."

"Rats!" interrupted Hugh.

Jabal smiled at him and said quietly, "You spoke as if you were confessing a dreadful sin."

"Well, I didn't mean to. I'm not ashamed of it." Hugh tossed his dark hair.

"Of course not," said Jabal. "Why should you be? There are still a few people, Mr Fuller, who have the mistaken idea that those who do not believe in the Christian God are for that reason immoral, dishonest, thieves or desperados, but I assure you it is not the general view of the clergy. It's not unbelievers who do harm. It's the believers, believers in strange cults and new sects which bring huge profits to

210

their organisers, and believers in gods who demand vengeance and condone cruelty. The Old Testament is full of such believers and there are too many in the world today. Those committing atrocities in Northern Ireland claim it is in the cause of their religion. They have the infernal impertinence to label their struggle 'a holy war' — a blatant contradiction in terms. They are the dangerous believers. They are the ones who should feel shame. There is never any need to explain, or apologise for, a lack of belief."

Hugh was looking at Jabal with amazement and, it seemed, more friendliness. He sat down again, his prepared speech over, then said. "Mary told us you took away that silly notice saying *coffin to let*. That was decent of you."

They were all looking at him with approval now. "Yes, I removed it," he admitted. "Which of you wrote it?"

The question was unexpected. It brought a quick denial from the

Martins. "We didn't." — "Not Cecil or me."

Daphne was the next to speak. "Stupid," she pronounced. "That's what it was. Stupid."

"Did the murderer do it?" asked Mary. "Was it a warning? Are we all going to be picked off one by one?" She was trying to speak lightly and deceived no one.

Denis turned to her. "Of course it wasn't a warning. It was an ill-timed attempt at humour by some passing student, that's all."

"I quite agree," said Mrs Dibbett. "In very bad taste. This house must be known as the scene of three deaths and he was trying to be witty. I think we should just forget it."

"None of us did it, Mr Jarrett," said Denis. "We've talked about it. But it was upsetting for the girls. Have you found any accommodation for them? That's our main concern at the moment."

"I couldn't finalise things without

your consent," Jabal told him. "But I've spoken to some members of the Ladies Guild and several would be willing to provide a room for a few weeks. That would give you time to look around for something more permanent. How many of you would be interested?"

There was no sudden response. Then Mrs Dibbett said, "It was very kind of you to take the trouble. I suppose we'll all have to go somewhere."

Then came a general murmur. "Yeah, thanks," from Daphne. "Indeed it was," from Denis. Grunts from the others. Then Hugh said, "We talked it over when Mary told us of your offer. If Tom and Josie hadn't been . . . I mean, if circumstances were normal, we'd none of us want to move just because the landlord had died and the place might be sold. We'd prefer to stay on and risk being given notice."

Cecil Martin began, "The Council ought to do something. It's really disgusting to leave us here with nowhere to go. It's not right. It's . . . "

No one looked at him and no one appeared to listen. It must be the practice to ignore the Martins, except to pity them and at times to help, as if they were pathetic animals to which one must not be unkind. Daphne had interrupted, "You see, we've done up our rooms here." She looked round Mary's. "Well, some of us have. Old Clagg wouldn't redecorate so we did it ourselves. Bought curtains and things — you know? And Hugh's repainted the whole of his."

Denis grinned. "If Mr Jarrett saw Hugh's, Daphne, he'd more likely assume a compelling urge on our part to leave the neighbourhood."

"Well *I* like it," said Hugh, "and I'm the one that lives in it. Come on up afterwards, Mr Jarrett, and I'll show you."

"Why not now? It'll give the others an opportunity to talk over my offer and make up their minds."

Hugh jumped to his feet and he and Jabal left the room. As they walked up the stairs Hugh said, "Don't you reckon the girls and Mrs Dibbett ought to go?"

"I don't think their safety depends on it," Jabal answered. "The house is under police protection."

"Yes, I know, but they're so scared. The girls, that is. Mrs Dibbett is standing it well enough. Surprising, that. Daph and Mary are all jittery and nervous and look as if they haven't slept for a week. They probably haven't, either. Well, here's my room." He threw open the door and gestured Jabal to enter. "Maybe you'd better sit down to admire it." He brought forward a chair.

Jabal laughed. "I'd better sit down to recover from the shock." He took the chair offered and gazed around him. The wall by the window, above the sink bench and small stove, had painted on it what looked like the parts of a car engine which would be strewn on the ground after a collision with an express train. But not of the same colour.

Nothing so dull. Green nuts, green bolts, a radiator cap of red and purple stripes a pink piston rod with a blue spotted ribbon tied round it in a bow. The adjacent wall was a dazzling mass of white geometric forms on a black background, with fine spirals whirling into a centre point, parallel curves dizzily weaving through converging straight lines, triangles, hexagons and various unidentifiable figures tangled together. As an inducement to an epileptic seizure it was superb. On the third wall was a startling scene of a tropical forest, with brilliantly coloured flowers and birds amid intertwining foliage. The door, in the middle of it, displayed an enormous, grinning peacock, the fourth wall, round the bricked-up fireplace, was painted a plain vivid yellow. The plastered bricks in the grate were decorated with orange spots. The brightly polished brass fender round the hearth looked out of place, but perhaps polished brass was the 'in' thing among Hugh's friends.

"Frighten you?" asked Hugh cheerfully. "I find it rather soothing myself, especially now."

"If it has that effect on you," said Jabal, "I'm fully in favour of it. And I can honestly say I like your fender. As you pointed out, it's you who lives in the room." He twisted his chair slightly to avoid facing the black and white wall. The car engine parts were preferable. He noticed the sink bench and stove beneath them were clean and uncluttered. "I'm glad it gives you some comfort. This must be an alarming time for you all."

"Yes, it is, but oddly it's not as bad now as it was at first. I think we've just had too many shocks. I guess there's a stage where you slide into a sort of torpor. An artificial calm, an anodyne bestowed by Nature, making us lethargic and numbed. Perhaps in the same way that a little bunny rabbit is unable to scamper away when it's being stared at by a weasel. Nature saying, 'Hold on, fellow, you've got to be eaten. Sorry about that, but it's all part of what people call my Balance. I'll make it easy for you. Just sit still and don't think about it.' See what I mean?"

"Yes, I think I do. But do the others feel the same?"

"It's hard to know, but that's the impression I get. The Martins don't care much about anyone else — other people can get themselves killed if they want to. No, that's not fair. They *are* upset and now and then, when they realise they could be in danger themselves, they get quite panicky. Denis — he's really deeply disturbed. He doesn't show it, for the sake of the rest of us, and he concentrates on the necessity of finding the killer in order to prevent any further deaths. Mrs Dibbett is amazingly calm about it all. The girls — well, they don't seem able to take it in sometimes. Other times you can see they've been howling, poor kids. I do hope you can get them out of it. But we're all, as I said, sort of stunned now and not suffering as much as an outsider might think. I feel we'll collapse later, when it's all over. In the meantime, we're managing to stand it."

"And how do these murals help you?"

"Well, let me explain . . . "

It was a quarter of an hour later that Jabal and Hugh rejoined the others. Denis said, "We were beginning to think Mr Jarrett had been knocked senseless by his surroundings. How did the sight affect you, Mr Jarrett?"

"In the words of Jeremiah, *all my bones shake; I am like a man whom wine hath overcome*."

"I can quite believe it," said Denis. "Well, we've talked over your very kind offer and we all think it would be wise to accept, thank you."

"Only because we're scared of what might happen next," said Daphne. "If the police would hurry up and find out who's killing people, we wouldn't go until we were actually given notice."

"But it's dreadful," moaned Vera. "They ought to arrest someone and take him away. It's not right to leave him here."

"It might be a woman," Daphne reminded her. "It might be you," she added unkindly.

Vera gave an indignant squeak and Cecil began to protest. "You have no right at all . . ."

Jabal thought it expedient to interrupt. "The police will find the killer in due course. I hope it will be soon. But haven't you any theories of your own in the matter?"

"There was silence as they looked at one another, each waiting for someone else to speak. Jabal went on, "I'm sure you've discussed it among yourselves. Did you come up with any ideas?"

Mary said, "We think it must be some maniac but we don't know why he should pick on this house in particular. Josie said she had a theory about Mr Clagg's death, but she didn't say what. I guess she knew more about street gangs than we do."

"It's scary," said Daphne. "Whose turn is next? That's what gets us." Like Mary, she was trying to speak casually but was unable to hide the tremor in her voice. "Is he lurking round out there, waiting for a chance to sneak in and kill someone else? The police put a chain on the front door for us but we all lock our own doors now, even in the daytime when we're home."

"You are wise to do so," said Jabal. "So you think it was a stranger who killed three residents here?"

"We want to think so," said Denis. "But we're not complete idiots. We know it could've been one of us. One of us here in this room right now." But he avoided looking at anyone except Jabal.

"Oh dear," said Mrs Dibbett. "I hardly think that would be so, Denis. You're all such nice people."

"The ones who caused dissension

are the ones who are gone," Denis pointed out. "Clagg, Josie and Tom. Is that coincidence? They were the ones disliked, or the ones who had rows with others. So who got rid of them?" This time he did look round the room at each in turn but not keeping his eyes on any one longer than another.

Jabal was inclined to agree with him but he could not announce 'One of you is a murderer'. He had made such a statement on previous occasions but then he had been sure it was so. Here he was not. An outsider *could* have been responsible. Yet they should be warned not to trust one another blindly. He too was looking round the room, examining each in turn, but knowing from past experience that one can seldom identify a murderer by his appearance or read character rightly from a facial expression. He said, "It might help to discuss it. You may know something useful without being aware of it, something you heard or saw which seemed unimportant at the time but which could in fact provide a lead."

Hugh laughed aloud and looked at the others. "Told you so!"

Mary explained to Jabal, "Hugh says he's heard of you and that you go round solving murders. Someone at Varsity told him."

Jabal smiled. "I assure you I do *not* 'go round solving murders'. A vicar's duties are much more mundane. It's true I've been involved in a few enquiries, but that has been mainly accidental. You may solve this particular problem yourselves. Suppose you tell me exactly what happened in each case? Significant facts may emerge. What about Mr Clagg? Who found him?" He already knew the facts but it could be useful to hear their versions.

Denis answered. "Tom Solley did."

"Which of you was the last to see him alive?"

"I guess I was," said Hugh. "I went in to pay my rent. We used to put it in a cash box there, with a note of our name."

"At what time was that?"

"About five. Solley found him at half past, so someone must've broken in during that half hour. The police said he hadn't been dead long when they arrived. Solley rang them on Clagg's phone and he shouldn't have because of prints, but how was he to know that? Anyway, they were here in a few minutes. Later we were asked to go in each in turn to see if we knew what was missing. There was a terrible mess all over the floor. Mostly broken crockery and food. And a few things had gone off the mantelpiece and the cash box was empty."

"Had none of you heard any noise from the flat?"

"No, but there's so much traffic at that time."

"How many of you were in the house?"

They looked at one another. Hugh said, "That's what the police keep asking. We were all home except Mary, but some of us had just come in and none of us can prove we were out when the killing took place."

"Vera and I were having our tea," said Cecil. "We didn't know anything about it."

Daphne gave him an impatient look. "None of us can say exactly where we were or when we got home that day. We tried to remember but we weren't sure."

Jabal had been shown by the inspector a list of times and places, obtained by questioning, but only the Martins had claimed to be sure of their facts. Why had the killer not taken the precaution to arrange an alibi? He said, "Have any of you something to add? Anything you noticed at the time that might help the police?"

There was silence. Then Mary said, "Josie was next. Here, in this very room."

"No she died in her own flat," said Daphne. "Hugh and I went in to see if she was all right because she'd felt sick and rushed out and there she was, all . . . oh, it was beastly."

"You phoned the police?"

"No. Hugh went out and told the nearest constable. He contacted Central on his radio-telephone and hordes of police cars arrived . . . "

"Three, dear," put in Mrs Dibbett.

"They said Josie had been poisoned and Tom said they accused him of not glazing a mug properly but that wasn't it because Josie had brought one of her own and it wasn't one of Tom's make. So Tom was furious and was rude to the police and they had it in for him after that."

Jabal didn't bother to correct this statement. C.I.B. men are well used to an angry reaction from those they interview and are understanding of the emotional disturbance that causes it.

Daphne continued, "It seemed that only Tom could have poisoned her because he dished out the coffee but now it looks as if he didn't because he was killed too."

Mary said, "I think any of us had as much chance as Tom did. Most of us walked about the room. Well, all of us except Vera and Cecil and they were sitting right next to her. I'm not saying that means anything," she added, as Vera began to squeak a protest. "I'm just explaining to Mr Jarrett how it was. Any one of us *could* have slipped poison into Josie's mug."

"But where would we get it from?" demanded Daphne. "Tom was the only one who had it. Gosh, the police were thorough, though. They searched all our rooms and took samples of everything."

"They took Cecil's migraine tablets," said Vera, "and my morning sickness pills. It's not fair. I had to go and get some more and it cost me four dollars. The police ought to pay."

"And in *my* room they found cannabis," said Hugh, "and took it all away."

"So they should've," said Daphne. "You said you weren't smoking it any more."

"Neither I am. But I hadn't thrown it out and they snarled and took it with them and looked daggers at me and now they regard me as chief suspect."

"Not necessarily," said Denis. "We all had tablets or medicaments of some sort. They left me the bottle with the repeat notice but took the contents. That was fair enough, they have to test everything. It's their job. The labels may have been false. Did you have only cannabis, Hugh?"

"No, I had some pills, and they left me the bottle too, but I'm damned if I'll get a repeat and pay for it. I don't need them anyway. I'm quite all right without. And they won't find poison in any of the stuff they confiscated, I bet."

"Of course not," agreed Daphne. "We think it must have been one of the men who used to come to Josie that killed her."

"We do *not*," protested Mary.

Mrs Dibbett suddenly spoke up. She had been very quiet. "No, you must not pretend, Daphne, dear. If Mr Jarrett is to help us in this dreadful matter we must tell him the exact truth, isn't that so, vicar? What was that verse you quoted to me the other day, something St Paul said about being truthful?" She looked the picture of sweet innocence.

You crafty old liar, thought Jabal, but replied. "Paul often advocated the truth, Mrs Dibbett. Was it *Shun profane and vain babblings?*"

"No, not that one, but it meant the same thing. So do as St Paul advised, Daphne."

Hugh laughed aloud. "I bet she's never heard of St Paul, have you, Daph?"

"I have so. He was one of those things on the end of a teaspoon."

"An apostle," said Jabal. "His advice to speak the truth was sound but I doubt if you and Hugh would approve his anti-feminist views."

"Daphne doesn't approve any anti-feminists," said Denis. "It's partly her Rights for Women adherance that stops her from even thinking of going to church." He smiled at her. "She told me once that she'd go to church when the clergy start calling God 'She' instead of 'He'."

"That could be arranged," said Jabal mildly, "providing we extend the same courtesy to the devil. Satan might be offended if we use the wrong pronoun for her."

Hugh burst out laughing again. He seemed in high spirits now. "Good for you, Vicar!"

Jabal turned to Denis. "I believe you were the one to find Mr Solley?"

"Yes. It was rather grim. I'd gone in to see if he'd come and have a cup of tea with the girls and me. I told you the other day."

"I know. But go over it again, will you?"

Denis looked puzzled but did as he was asked. His account did not differ from that of the previous occasion, but not all the others had heard it in detail.

"You looked to see where we were?" demanded Hugh. "The bloody cheek!"

"It was to give you all an alibi," said Mary.

"The truth, dear," Mrs Dibbett reminded her.

"Well, it was partly that. We didn't think you'd done it, Hugh. Not for a moment." Her eyes pleaded with him. "Denis just suggested we check up on everyone before we rang the police, so we could support any statements you made later about where you were at the time."

"We needn't have bothered," said Hugh, now scowling. "I'm their chief suspect for that, too, because of all the fights I had with Tom."

Cecil said, "Denis had a fight with him too."

"That just shows how bad-tempered Tom was," said Mary.

Denis disagreed. "It was understandable in my case. He was doing very delicate work at the time and I shouldn't have chosen that moment to upset him. I don't think he meant to hurt me. He just picked up a knife and slashed out in a sort of absent-minded way, like killing a mosquito."

"I think you're very generous to talk like that about an attempt to kill you," said Mary. "Did you have to tell the police about it?"

"They already knew. Someone else had told them. I just filled in a few details. So you see, Hugh, I could equally well be the chief suspect."

The discussion continued. There were no accusations, not even significant looks at one person. Hugh had become quiet and sulky, saying nothing. The Martins looked frightened but subdued. Mrs Dibbett looked down at her folded hands. Daphne had begun biting one finger nail. Yet it was clear to Jabal that most of them could still not accept the fact that one of them sitting there was a person to beware of, a killer of three others. They were frightened, but not of one another. The human mind often believes what it most wants to believe and they were obstinately clinging to the hope that an outsider — or three outsiders — had committed the murders. Such an attitude was dangerous.

In the end he rose. "If any of you thinks of something that would help, do please let the police know. If you don't want to speak to the police, you are welcome to phone me at any time. My number's in the book. You must face the fact that one of you here may be a murderer." He paused to see how they took this, but there was no noticeable reaction. In their hearts they must know it to be true. "For that reason, I advise you not to discuss the killings any more among yourselves. Be alert, watch, listen, but don't talk about it. Say nothing to upset one another. In such times of stress it is easy to make an injudicious remark or let an argument get out of hand. In the words of St James, *Let every man be swift to hear, slow to speak, slow to wrath.* He turned to Daphne. "James was another . . . er . . . thing on the end of a teaspoon. Now that I know what you want, I'll see my parishioners again and arrange some definite proposals to put to you regarding accommodation."

He left then. As he walked back to his car and drove home to the vicarage, he again had the feeling that he had been informed of the identity of the murderer and had been too unreceptive to see it. He went over the conversation trying to recall every word spoken and by whom. It was a good mental exercise but told him nothing.

11

JABAL did as he had promised. He took names and addresses of those of his parishioners who were willing to house a tenant of Fairway Flats and noted down the dates on which their accommodation would be available. But which of them would then be lodging a murderer? While there was any risk that one of these good ladies might be knifed, poisoned or brained, he was not prepared to finalise arrangements, so he deferred another visit to the flats.

His talk with the residents there had given him a superficial idea of the character of each, or of the character which each wished to project, and he could see none of them in the role of triple murderer. Several lies had been told. No, no, one must not prejudge. Several statements had been made which were *probably* lies. Why would a man who worked at a supermarket be having his tea at home at five thirty? What was a shop assistant doing arriving home at that hour on a late shopping night? Did they imagine that since an outside door had been forced, being *inside* the house gave them an alibi? And would a man who had smoked marijuana and then given it up, retain the drug for several years in a small room where space was limited? Had Denis Day really found nothing suspicious when he checked the tenants' whereabouts? Was his account of his quarrel with Solley an accurate one? Had Josie Wallace really told the Grayson girl that she had a theory about Clagg's death? Would Vera Martin bother to buy more morning sickness pills if she had to pay for them herself? Had none of them altered the land agent's sign? Lies had surely been told, but all men lie and often for the most trivial of reasons.

Three days after Jabal's visit to the flats, Inspector Chambers phoned him. "They've identified the poison that killed Wallace. It was barium carbonate, a material used in some pottery glazes."

"Then it came from Solley's stock?"

"It looks that way. But that doesn't mean he administered it. It's usually in the form of a white powder. Only a few grams will cause death in fifteen minutes, the lab boys say. There were two cases last year of accidental poisoning of children playing in their father's studio. Nearly fatal in each case. You know, Jabal, there are no regulations governing the use of poisons in studio potteries. It's ridiculous. It makes me mad. But to get back to Wallace — she took a white mug along that evening for her coffee, so the powder could already be in it. All the tenants had access to Solley's rooms and this was one jar labelled correctly."

"But who would know it was poisonous?"

"That's the question. None of them works in any place where it would be used or even known. It's not a common poison. Which brings us back to Solley. Unless Solley explained its properties to one of the others, and why should he do that?"

"He could very well do that. He liked talking about his work and his glazes. But although the tenants had access to his flat, they didn't have access to Miss Wallace's. Besides, how would anyone know she would take that particular mug to the coffee gathering?"

"They didn't. They were prepared to wait. Therefore it was not someone who had an urgent need to dispose of her but someone with a deep-seated hatred."

"Is that what you believe, Trevor?"

"No Jabe, it's not. It doesn't explain the other deaths, unless the murderer killed Solley to prevent him from disclosing the name of the person to whom he'd given information about barium carbonate. And what's all that got to do with Clagg?"

"Miss Grayson told me that Miss Wallace said she had a theory about Clagg's death."

"So have I. So, no doubt, have you, and all the tenants. I gather she didn't say what her theory was? It would be an understandable remark to make in conversation. If she had some knowledge that the others didn't, wouldn't she have been more specific? I suppose it's possible she knew who killed Clagg, or guessed. If she was then stupid enough to approach that person with an accusation, he couldn't afford to wait. And the only one who would know where to obtain poison in a hurry would be Solley. It all comes back to him, every time. He dished out the coffee and it would take only a second or two to drop poison in her cup. Someone saw him doing it and protested by way of bashing his brains in."

"It would've been simpler to inform the police. Trevor, how accurately can one estimate the time of a death?"

"You're thinking that if Solley's were later than supposed, those three who were in Grayson's flat would have an alibi? Well, it's not an easy matter. The man Day found the body and his estimate actually accords with that of the police surgeon but they may both be wrong. If a qualified pathologist examines a body within ten minutes of death, time of death can be estimated to within a minute or two. Within half an hour, it can be estimated to within ten minutes either way. The longer the interval, the greater the margin of error. And so many factors have to be taken into account — even amount of food recently taken and stage of digestion, which of course is not known until the autopsy."

"Will the tenants be informed as to what poison was used for Wallace?"

"Unless Solley was the poisoner, one of them already knows. No, I don't intend to tell them or to release it to the press. I'd prefer the killer not to know it's been identified. I want him off guard, confident that he's got away with it. But we'll have to question them all further. Just thought you'd like the latest information." Trevor hung up.

Jabal sat for a while thinking after he had replaced the receiver. Solley had the best opportunity to poison Josie, but why should he do so? He didn't want her in the house but he'd put up with the situation for four or five years. What would trigger off a sudden desire to kill her? The fact that she knew he had killed Clagg? But Solley had not wanted Clagg out of the way. Far from it. He was sitting pretty with his kiln and his wheel set up so near the market. And why was Solley himself killed? It was more likely that he knew who killed both Clagg and Josie and unwisely made an accusation . . .

Jabal was still trying to sort some logic and order into what seemed a tangle of unrelated facts when he saw a man and a boy walking up his path. George Simmons and his son Charlie.

The boy was crying.

He opened his study door before they needed to knock. "Come in, Mr Simmons. Is something wrong? What's the trouble, Charlie?"

Mr Simmons pushed his son in, glared at him with paternal wrath and said, "Come on, boy. Tell the vicar."

The youngster, about ten years old, lifted a tear-stained face. "But I didn't do it. Honest I didn't. It wasn't me that made them sound different."

"You meant to," growled his father. "Vicar, that change in the hymn numbers last Sunday . . . "

"Charlie didn't do that." Young Keith Merton had already been forced into a confession of perpetrating the misdeed. He had climbed up while the church was empty and altered the number of the third hymn on the list. As a consequence the congregation were briefly puzzled as to how they could exhort holy angels bright to hark their song while half a dozen organ pipes were, with more volume, enquiring into the movement of feet in ancient time. But they had quickly ceded victory to the organ, found the right page in their books, and the prank had fallen flat.

"The boy's mouth dropped open. "You know who done it?"

"Yes. One of your young friends has admitted to it. The matter is over and done with."

"Not quite it isn't." Mr Simmons prodded his son. "Come along, Charles."

Charlie hesitated, then dropped his head and mumbled, "Dad says I gotta tell you I did it first, only someone musta found out, 'cos it was changed back."

"Yes, it was changed twice. Mr Bailey noticed it the first time and corrected it." The curate had reported to Jabal in indignation this unwarranted interference with the morning's bill of fare, and had added a few bitter remarks about the deplorable behaviour of today's youth.

"So you did it the first time?" asked

Jabal and tried to look stern. "Why did you do it?"

The boy looked up, distress in his eyes. "Squibby Merton dared me to. And I *did* and he won't believe me." His father gave him another nudge and he added hurriedly, "I know it was wrong and I'm very sorry and I won't ever do it again."

Poor child. He was a timid boy. He had actually screwed up enough courage to carry out the dare and the curate had sabotaged his effort. His friend Squibby had not believed he'd done it and to prove himself the better man had changed the numbers himself. No wonder Charlie was upset. The problems of a ten-year-old can be devastating. To be accused of chickening out by his friend, who would not only taunt him but would tell all their mates . . . Jabal took pity. Assuming a severe expression, he said, "It was very wrong of you to change the hymn numbers, Charlie. You should be punished. Keith Merton has owned up and been reprimanded. But as for you . . . let me see . . . I feel that, as punishment, I must announce to the assembled Junior Youth Group next Saturday that you were originally responsible for changing the numbers and that Mr Bailey saw what had been done and changed them back."

He saw the boy's eyes light up. Poor little fellow.

"Public humiliation," agreed Mr Simmons. "That's the ticket."

"I hope you will consider it sufficient punishment, Mr Simmons. There's no need for further action and I'm sure Charlie will never do it again." No, God willing, he'd now have the courage for bigger and better deeds, something more enterprising. He'd forced himself into doing what he feared to do and on Saturday he'd have proved himself in the eyes of his friends. An important step in the difficult process of growing up.

"You'll denounce him in front of all the other boys?" asked Mr Simmons.

"I'll make a point of it."

"And that'll serve you right, my lad," said Mr Simmons. "I just hope it teaches you a lesson. Come on, we mustn't waste any more of Mr Jarrett's time. Thank you, vicar."

Jabal showed them out and watched them go through the front gate. Was there a little more confidence in the boy's bearing? He liked to think so.

His mind went back to the Fairway Flats problem, where had he got to? Let's see . . . someone robbed Clagg, killing him when he unexpectedly walked in, Josie Wallace knew who it was, announced that she 'had a theory' and therefore had to be removed. Solley knew who killed Josie, so *he* had to be . . . oh, nonsense! utter nonsense. There was no apparent motive for any of the killings. The face of young Charlie Simmons kept interrupting Jabal's thoughts. There had been something about that interview with the boy, something that reminded him . . . of what? Of another occasion. Some time, some where, it had happened before. Then it came to him. The boy, lifting a tearful face. 'I didn't do it. Honest I didn't.' And an old lady, sitting primly in the same study. 'I didn't kill him, you see.'

She'd actually said that Clagg was 'better out of the way'. But Josie? Why would she want to kill Josie? She'd called Josie 'good-natured' and 'generous' and that was the way Josie had impressed him, too. Honest, as well. Suddenly, in the whirl of confusing thoughts and memories, Jabal recalled one small piece of information he had been given two weeks ago.

Half an hour later he was ringing the front door bell of Fairway Flats. It was Mrs Dibbett herself who opened the door. "Oh, come in, vicar. How nice to see you. I was so surprised when you telephoned to see if I would be in. It really is good of you to take so much trouble."

Jabal unceremoniously cut her short. "I want to speak to you, Mrs Dibbett.

Let's go into your flat."

When they were seated, he came straight to the point. "Now tell me the truth. When you decided to kill Mr Clagg, what method did you intend to use?"

"Oh, vicar, how can you say such a thing! I didn't kill poor Mr Clagg."

"But you meant to. You planned to."

"Why I wouldn't . . . "

"I want the truth, Mrs Dibbett, and I want it now." Jabal's face was at its sternest and his grey eyes searching. Even a soul as stout as that of Mrs Dibbett found it difficult to withstand his keen, piercing glance.

"You . . . know?" she faltered.

"Yes, I know. It was very, very wrong of you."

"Oh, but he was not a nice man, vicar. Moses thought it right that bad men should be put to death."

Jabal sighed and not for the first time wondered why the complete version of the Old Testament was made available to all and sundry. There was so much in it that was excellent, but all tangled up with tales of lust, cruelty and revenge, approved or ordered by, blood-thirsty gods. How could the man in the street be expected to sort out the mess?

Miss Dibbett misinterpreted his silence. "So I knew it was a good thing to do," she went on, "since Moses said so."

Moses had been a cunning, intelligent old codger who adapted his teaching to the needs of his times and the superstitions of his people. Men are no less gullible now, but circumstances have changed. A Moses of today would never get away with a story of a hibiscus bush in the Domain bursting into flames and remaining intact. Nor of being handed a new set of by-laws on the top of Mt Eden by a fellow bathed in neon light. He'd have to claim they were dropped from a U.F.O. or spewed out by the super power of a highly advanced technical robot. The populace might buy it in that form.

"What's the matter, vicar? You look upset."

Jabal roused himself. "I *am* upset, Mrs Dibbett. Any pronouncement Moses gave about eliminating murderers and evil criminals, was meant as a drastic form of punishment to be decided on by the authorities of a community. Never, never, did he advocate the taking of one individual's life by another. *Thou shalt not kill*, remember? What you intended to do was contrary to all his precepts. It was very, very wicked . . . "

For a quarter of an hour he reasoned, preached, reprimanded and deplored. Mrs Dibbett tried her best to look repentant because she thought it would please the vicar and she liked to give pleasure to others. When he became too uncomfortably reproachful she let her mind wander. She was disappointed that she had not been the instrument of Mr Clagg's removal herself. Her plan would've worked in time if those vandals hadn't broken in. It had been a good plan. Not as good as burning oleander leaves of course, but there just hadn't been the opportunity of a barbecue, or any oleander leaves in the street. And the arrangements she'd made would've ensured a quick death. Much better than sticking a knife in the poor man's back. She did hope that hadn't hurt him too much . . .

"Mrs Dibbett! Are you listening to me?"

"Why yes, vicar, of course I am. So kind of you to explain." She turned her eyes to him meekly.

He looked at her fiercely. "Then tell me — and I want the truth! — just how were you going to kill Mr Clagg?"

12

MARY GRAYSON turned wearily in at the gate. It was decent of them to let her come home at four. Mrs Kirby, it was. Concerned at the look of Mary, she'd had a word with the floorwalker, who'd gone up to Management and come back to send her home. No cut in pay, either. The Farmers were a good firm to work for. Like giving you Friday nights off sometimes when you worked Saturday.

She put her key in the front door but the chain was on. That chain was a protection and a nuisance. Didn't the police realise what it would involve, with so many of them using the front entrance? It was more often than not left unfastened. She rang the bell and after a few moments heard steps shuffling down the stairs. Cecil Martin peered out at her, then released the door. So that was why the chain had been fastened. Timid, frightened Cecil had been the last one in.

"You're early," he remarked.

"So are you, Cecil. What are you doing home at this hour?" The poor man looked pale and exhausted.

"I've been thinking." Just the sort of reply he would make. Did he so seldom think that he had to come home to indulge in the hobby? It wasn't the first time he'd been home during the day. He'd opened the door to her when she had a lift home for lunch last Wednesday. She had a sudden suspicion and asked him directly, "You *are* still working at the supermarket, aren't you?"

"Why wouldn't I be? Of course I . . . " he stopped. His mouth worked silently, his eyebrows twitched, then he said. "Can I talk to you, Mary. I've been thinking."

"Come in." He followed her into her flat and flopped down on the couch. Like a dead fish. But gosh, you couldn't help feeling sorry for him. Just to *look* like he did was bad enough. "Cecil, you're not working are you? You're out of a job."

"It wasn't my fault, Mary. I hadn't actually taken the things. They admitted that, but they said they had to cut down and last in first out. I wasn't entitled to any redundancy pay but they gave me a cheque all the same."

"So you're on the unemployment benefit? How long has it been?"

"Three weeks. Don't tell the others, will you? If Mr Clagg had found out he'd've given us notice because he'd know the dole isn't enough for the rent he charged and everything else as well. We've just been managing on what we'd saved and the cheque they gave me."

"No wonder you were looking for another place. It wasn't just the baby coming?"

"Well, it was that too. He'd have thrown us out for one reason or the other. I've been looking for a job each day, Mary, but they all turn me down. The Labour Department keeps giving me names of firms to try but it's never any good. One fellow said I looked as if I was afraid of work. He didn't even give me a chance. They none of them do. And I'm *not* afraid. It isn't fair. I'm quite strong, you know, and I'm *not* afraid to do things. Vera and I used to go to church, you know. I wasn't just *saying* that the other day. We really did."

Mary suppressed a smile. She had not regarded attending church an act of courage.

"So I know. And I'm going to ask him this evening, I'm going to ask him. I'm not afraid to do that. That chap had no right to say I look afraid." He thrust forward what he had of a chin and set his lips.

"Of course not," said Mary. But who *would* employ him? There were so many applicants now for employers to choose from. She had a sudden idea.

255

"I know, Cecil! Grow a beard."

"What?"

"Do you remember how we were talking about beards that day the vicar was here? And why people have them? One would alter your appearance no end. Make you look more experienced, I think. You're hair's dark and your beard would be rather attractive."

Cecil was fingering his chin. "You reckon? I wonder how long it would take? I'll ask Vera what she thinks. I'll go and do it now." He got up.

"What did you want to talk to me about Cecil?"

"Oh. That. It can wait. That's a very good idea about the beard, I'm going to go and tell Vera. Thanks, Mary."

He left her and she heard his steps rapidly mount the stairs. Poor, silly Cecil. A beard might help though. He'd still be as wet but he mightn't look it. She kicked off her shoes before she switched on the kettle. She was more than usually tired. She wandered over to the window and looked out on the traffic. She suddenly hated the constant stream of cars past the house, the dusty greyness of the street, the squeal of tyres. It was all so impersonal and uncaring, especially to one like herself who'd been brought up in a small town like Paeroa, where everyone knew everyone. No one even looked at you in Symonds Street. They didn't care enough. They didn't smile, they didn't speak, they didn't realise you were there unless they paused to look on with a mild interest while you were being mugged and screaming for help. Hostile strangers passing by. You hardly saw the same person twice.

It hadn't always been so bad. She used to enjoy the bustle and constant activity. Perhaps it was a passing mood and a cup of strong tea would shake her out of it. It hadn't really been a bad day — just that woman complaining because they didn't stock left-handed nail scissors — as though it was Mary's fault! — and Heather getting shaky about the change of lunch hours. But on the whole no worse than usual. Her mind simply hadn't been on her work and it was hard to take an interest in any customers. Frightened? Yes, she was. She had to admit it. Daph was, too. She guessed the men were also a bit scared but it wasn't manly to show it. Funny, though — Cecil hadn't seemed scared. Just worried over having no job and nowhere to move to. Poor Cecil. How was old Mrs Dibbett feeling about it all? Three murders! It still seemed unbelievable. When would she wake up? Better if she didn't. Better this odd daze, this inability to think straight, this automatic carrying out of everyday chores and habits. If her head did clear, if she woke up and grasped fully the horror of what had happend, she felt she would scream . . . and scream . . . and scream . . .

She made her tea and sank into a chair to drink it. Emotional stress and fear and confused thoughts were exhausting. She hoped that vicar chap would find them all somewhere else to live — that is, if it didn't mean losing contact with Hugh. That was the trouble. Come on, girl, face it. Be honest. It was being separated from Hugh that she dreaded most. Not that *he* cared. If only they'd arrest someone and end it all. But who? It couldn't be anyone in the house, it simply couldn't. If only she could think lucidly, she could decide what she ought to do. Her parents were frantic, phoning and urging her to go home and threatening to come and fetch her forcibly if she didn't. But she wouldn't get a job in Paeroa and she was darned if she'd go on the dole and be labelled a bludger.

The doorbell rang. Blast that chain. Cecil had fastened it again. She was the nearest. She'd better go. She got up reluctantly and went out to the hall, unthinkingly releasing the chain before she opened the door. But it was only Hugh. He looked ghastly, white, haggard, his eyes moving quickly. "Hugh, what's the matter?"

"Matter? Nothing. Why should there be?" He didn't even thank her for opening the door but turned to go upstairs.

"I've made a pot of tea. Like a cup?"

"No, thanks. I want to see Denis. There's something I want to ask him."

"I don't think he's home yet."

"Then I'll wait till he is." He walked away and up the stairs.

Mary went back into her room, this time leaving the chain off its catch. She'd get one of the men to remove it. Or do it herself. Mrs Dibbett had a screwdriver. She'd borrowed it once to retrieve an earring that had rolled under the skirting board.

Hugh had been very surly. He'd been different altogether lately. On edge. Well, they all were, of course. It was understandable. But Hugh was unlike himself. Having awful fits of depression and seeming really distraught at times. Of course he was so very sensitive, sensitive of other people's feelings as

260

well as his own. He felt things so deeply.

She heard the front door open, then Mrs Dibbbett's door open and close. Good thing she'd left the chain undone. Denis would be coming home soon too. He wouldn't need to ring. Why did Hugh want to see him? It was as though Hugh had something on his mind. Or as if he was inwardly fighting something. He reminded her of someone else . . . oh, that guy in Hardware who'd been an alcoholic and was trying to knock it. Going to A.A. He made no secret of it. The same change of moods. They'd kept him on, jolly decent of them too, and he swore he'd make the grade. Was Hugh secretly an alcoholic? He'd never given any signs of it. Yet the behaviour was the same. Withdrawal symptoms. Oh — the cannabis! The police had taken away the cannabis and he was still smoking it. Why else would he have kept it? Hugh had lied. He hadn't just tried it and then given it up. He was hooked on the stuff. Yet he dared not buy more while the police were investigating him. But why had he lied to *her*? He should've known she'd only want to help. Come to think about it, there was something else he'd lied about, too. That morning when Tom was killed. He'd been in his room yet he'd been going to go to an Anti-Fluoridation meeting, according to Daphne. Why had he stayed behind?

Hugh . . . Hugh had gone into Mr Clagg's room to leave his rent. Hugh was the last to see him alive. Now don't panic. Don't jump to conclusions. Think clearly . . . Josie . . . the morning Josie died. Hugh had taken round the jug of water and poured it into the cups. With a phial or a tablet in the other hand? It was just as easy for him as for Tom Solley. It was Hugh who'd said they all really wanted to get rid of Josie . . . and then not supported Mary when she repeated his words. It was Hugh who was constantly quarrelling with Tom Solley. Tom must've seen Hugh put poison in Josie's mug. Or

Hugh had taken poison from Tom's room and Tom had found out and Hugh knew Tom had found out so Tom had to be silenced before he could tell the police. Yes, it all fitted.

She'd really known all along and refused to let her mind accept it, because of the attraction he had for her. Now she began thinking of remarks Hugh had made, little things he had done. All confirmed his guilt. Hugh was the only one except the Martins who was hard up, the one who would have reason to steal from Mr Clagg ... maybe he didn't have the rent that week, the rent he said he'd gone in to deposit in the cashbox. And Mr Clagg had threatened him with eviction. And Josie guessed. She 'had a theory' and said so.

For a while Mary sat stunned, sickened. Then after the first shocked period of realisation, she experienced a strange wave of relief. She was freed. Freed from her desire for him, from the constant yearning for the unattainable. That was over now, over for good. Thank heaven. But she'd talked so freely with him, chattered away without thinking. Had she said something which made him realise that she would eventually work things out and know he was the killer? What would he do to her if he thought she suspected? She'd have to tell the police. But tell them what? She hadn't any proof. She just *knew*. They might not believe her and they might let *him* know what she'd said and . . . she shuddered. She could ring up the vicar bloke, though. She had an idea he'd listen more sympathetically. There was the phone. Ring him now. She forced herself to get up — hell, she was tired! — and turned the pages of the phone book. Here it is. St Bernard's church . . . vicar . . . She dialled the number with trembling fingers. There was no answer. She let it ring twenty times and then hung up. He was out. Just as well, perhaps. He might have got her into a corner and said 'Let us pray'.

She flopped back into her chair. She *might* try later. She heard the front door open again and another familiar tread through the hall. She sprang up and went out. 'Denis!' Reliable, imperturbable, dependable Denis. Always kind to her, always thoughtful and willing and considerate. She'd never really appreciated it as she should.

"Mary! What are you doing home so early? What is it? Is something wrong?"

"Come in. I've something to tell you." She pulled him into her flat.

Denis sat with her on the couch, holding her hand tightly, reassuringly, as she told him what she knew. His face was grave and he nodded at intervals but he did not interrupt. When she'd finished, she looked at him, looked into his serious, concerned eyes and knew she'd told him nothing. "Denis . . . you . . . you knew?"

"I didn't know, Mary, I suspected, but I had no proof. We still have none."

"How did you know?"

"He was the only one who could've done it. His temperament, for one thing. Can you imagine Cecil Martin smashing crockery in Clagg's flat? And Hugh resented Josie being here. He often told me so. Funny, how a murderer can be a prude in some respects. And you know he hated Tom."

"But why did he do it, Denis? After living here with them for years? Why now?"

"He was in debt and had to get money, especially for his rent. You know what Clagg was like. Never gave credit. Hugh would've been out on his ear. I'd lent him sums several times and — oh, Mary. I may be responsible for it all. Because the week Clagg was killed, I refused. I could've lent him more, it wasn't that I was short myself. But I didn't think it good to go on. If he had no job he could've gone to the Social Welfare and applied for the unemployment benefit. I felt it was up to him. He was gambling, did you know? That's where my money would've gone. He still is gambling and getting further and further into debt."

"And was it Josie saying she 'had a theory' that made him kill her?"

"I imagine so. I like to think it was partly under the influence of marijuana, while he didn't realise what he was doing."

"Is it really as powerful as that? And anyway he said he'd stopped."

"I know he did. But he couldn't hide its smell, not upstairs, where we're all so close. Did you ever wonder why, if he'd given it up, he still kept some in his flat?"

"Did Cecil Martin know?"

"Of course. The Martins could smell it. I bet the police did too."

"Hugh's waiting for you to come home. He said he wants to ask you something."

"For more money, I guess. To gamble with or to buy more pot. Poor devil."

"And Cecil let me in this afternoon and he said he was going to ask someone something this evening. He sounded mysterious and spoke as if he was being very brave."

"Did he give any indication who the 'someone' was?"

"No. He just said he used to go to church and so he knew and was going to ask someone. I don't know what he meant."

Denis's eyes narrowed. "Did he indeed? I hope he does nothing rash."

"I tried to ring Mr Jarrett later but he wasn't home. I didn't like to phone the police or speak to the constable because if they just laughed at me and Hugh found out what I'd done . . . "

His hands tightened on hers. "That's right. The police wouldn't listen. And *don't* ring the vicar. It would be a waste of time. We have no proof."

"Then what can we do?"

"I may have a talk with Hugh myself. If I tell him what we know . . . "

"Oh, no, Denis, that would be dangerous."

"It may be the only way. An accusation could bring interesting results. He may blurt out the truth. I'll be prepared for an attack and I'm as strong as he is. He must be practically out of his mind with all that preying on his conscience. He may even find some relief in knowing it's over."

"You sound as if you're almost sorry for him."

"I am. I'm sorry for anyone who has killed and I don't think Hugh was entirely responsible for his actions. I'll go now, Mary. Lock your door, and *don't leave the flat.*"

"Be careful, Denis."

When he had left she sat motionless, thinking. Hugh, the murderer, was just overhead. He must be living in fear, waiting, dreading, daily expecting to be arrested. No wonder he had dark hollows under his eyes. And she couldn't feel one scrap of sympathy for him.'

The whole situation was horrible, beastly . . . well, shattering, really. She mustn't think about it. Force her mind away. Yet, all the time, something was nagging at her memory, as if trying to push itself up into her consciousness. Like those subliminal tapes they were talking about and the ghastly things they could do to you in the way of brain washing. Something had been taped onto her unconscious and was struggling to rise to the surface. Something else Hugh had said or done? Another lie he'd told? A statement which didn't register as being false at the time, yet didn't sound quite right?

Don't think about it. Think of other things. Nice things. Work. Think of work and the friendly people there in Haberdashery. That woman hadn't been friendly, though. Silly old trout. She'd told her about the new left-hand shop opened and how to get there. It wasn't far away, it wouldn't have hurt her to walk a few yards. What did it matter, anyway? What was the difference in a pair of scissors? She'd thought they were all the same. It must be funny to be left-handed. The way they wrote, for instance. It would be easier for them to go from right to left. She remembered someone had shown her a left-hander's diary once, which started January 1st at the back. Poor old Tom Solley had been left-handed but that wouldn't matter in making pots. Or did he spin the wheel anti-clockwise? She'd never thought to ask him. What was it like? Combing your hair, for instance. She could see into the small hanging mirror from where she was sitting, so she raised her left hand and went through the motion of combing. To any left-hander it would be just the same. There was a smudge on her left cheek. Gosh, had she come home like that? Why hadn't Cecil or Denis *told* her? She rubbed it off, still using her left hand, then suddenly stopped, her hand still raised. She was rubbing the *right* cheek of the woman in the mirror. That was it! That was what had been nagging at her all this time. Oh God! If a left-handed man struck out with a knife he wouldn't wound someone's *left* temple. It would be the other one, the right.

She slowly lowered her hand. Denis had lied. *Denis*, not Hugh. Think back. Think over it all. Mr Clagg . . . Josie . . . Tom. Where had Denis been sitting at that coffee gathering? What had he taken round the room to offer people? He'd have had as much opportunity as Hugh, anyway. *Denis*! She could hardly believe it. Ah, but he couldn't have killed Tom because he was with her and Daphne at the time. Tom had been dead at least ten minutes when Denis found him, because Denis went in to his room at eleven and it was only twelve past when he rang the police. And *they* said he'd been dead at least half an hour. It had seemed much longer than twelve minutes that Denis had dithered around before he phoned them. How had he known it was eleven? For a long time Mary sat thinking, remembering, going over all the horrible events again trying to recall the details of each. Then she got up, as if in a daze and went across the hall. She had to know for certain. She knocked on Mrs Dibbett's door.

The old lady smiled when she opened the door and saw Mary. "Oh come in, my dear. Are you early home today? How nice."

Mary tried to speak calmly. "No I won't come in, thank you. I just wanted to ask you something. You go to church."

"And you'd like to come with me next Sunday? Why, of course. I *am* glad."

"No, no, Mrs Dibbett. I don't want to come. But would you mind telling me — the bells, the church bells. Why do they ring them?"

"To summon the faithful to worship, my dear. It's a very old custom. To let everyone know that the service will shortly begin."

"When do they *start* ringing them?"

"Well it varies. About a quarter of an hour before the service, generally. If they have a good team of ringers, it can be as much as half an hour before."

"Thank you, Mrs Dibbett." Mary turned away and went quickly back into her own flat.

Cecil Martin used to go to church. So, according to Cecil, he *knew*. And he was going to 'ask him' this evening. And Hugh had wanted to see Denis too. There was something *he* wanted to ask him. Both of them had guessed. Denis was strong, a match for Hugh and Cecil together, and he had said he was going up 'prepared'. She must do something. Interfere. Stop the encounter, the accusations, and the awful retaliatory fourth murder that might ensue. And Hugh! They mustn't hurt Hugh! She would stop it somehow.

With her heart pounding, she unlocked the door and went out into the hall again. Then she forced herself to begin walking up the stairs.

274

13

AT the time when Mary was trying to phone him, the vicar was at the Central Police Station, sitting in the office of Inspector Chambers.

"So that was it," said Trevor. "The crafty old devil!"

"If only I had remembered earlier that Josie Wallace had borrowed two mugs from Clagg! She told me so the day I met her. She liked the shape, she said, and wanted to keep them, provided she could pay for them. I applauded her honesty but forgot what she said and I blame myself bitterly for that."

"Well, don't. You couldn't have prevented her death because you weren't to know that the old lady had doctored one of them, and you couldn't predict that Wallace would take that particular one to the coffee

275

meeting in Grayson's flat."

"She told me she had borrowed the mugs but never used them. That must've been the first time — she probably gathered up this mug to take with her and didn't look carefully inside it."

"How did the old girl manage it?"

"Solley had let her inspect his glazes. She was interested in his pottery and he was always ready to talk about it. She looked up poisons in library books and decided on barium carbonate because it was obtainable from Solley's stock and because the book she read told her it was a rapid poison. Solley had said the same thing. She thought that meant rapid and painless, just the thing she was looking for, to do away with the landlord."

"But when Wallace was poisoned, didn't she have the least suspicion that it might be her fault?"

"I asked her that. Apparently the idea occurred to her briefly, then she discarded it because after Clagg was killed she'd looked in every cupboard of his flat to make absolutely sure the mug she fixed was not left intact. You gave her the opportunity for that when you asked the tenants in to estimate what was missing. She says there were white fragments on the floor so she assumed that mug had been smashed with all the other crockery and glass. Reasonable enough. And your people never made public the name of the poison used, so she had no reason to think she was responsible for her death. Actually, she sounded a little disappointed that someone else had killed Clagg. She imagined she was doing something useful, like Charlotte Corday stabbing Marat in his bath. I could not detect any genuine remorse, although she did her best to simulate it."

"It's a wonder Wallace didn't notice the stuff in the mug."

"She used a little icing off a cake to make the powder stick and then smoothed it over carefully until she achieved a uniformly even surface. She seems proud of her handiwork. She assured me no one could've noticed it was there. She took the mug one day when she went to pay her rent and sneaked it back the next. The idea was that sooner or later Clagg would use that mug. He didn't have visitors. A simple plan."

"You understand that Wallace's death was murder?"

"It was an accident. She liked Wallace and would be most distressed to know she was instrumental in her death."

"It was nevertheless murder, culpable homicide. I once threatened to quote from the Crimes Act, didn't I? Well here we are Page 707, Section 167, *Murder defined, Clause (c): If the offender means to cause death, or, being so reckless as aforesaid, means to cause such bodily injury as aforesaid to one person and by accident or mistake kills another person, though he does not mean to hurt the person killed.*

That's clear enough. If you ever quote one Bible verse too many and I draw a gun to shoot you and hit a passing typist by mistake, I am guilty of murder of the typist."

"Oh dear! Will she be charged?"

"Of course. She has murdered. But at the moment Solley's death takes precedence."

"Yes. I suppose so. Clagg was killed by intruders then, as you thought all along?"

"Everything pointed to it. The other deaths were what raised doubt about Clagg's. We could see no connection. But now . . . Wallace's death being an accident . . . Solley was killed in indignation or revenge because he was thought to have poisoned Wallace. We can bring a charge now."

"I suppose you've suspected the fellow all along?"

"Yes. His testimony was full of lies. But we couldn't connect him with the other two deaths. Now, thanks to you . . . "

"So what about Mrs Dibbett? Do you have to drag her in? You'll have one arrest."

"She is guilty of murder."

"She's seventy-eight. What good will it do to drag her through the ordeal of the court? Is there no way out of it?"

The inspector frowned. "Oh, I don't know, Jabal. I don't want to see her in the dock, any more than you do. At that age, to be put through the procedure of arrest, custody, and finally a trial — and then? Incarceration or, if her counsel presses for it and succeeds, detention in a mental institution. But I don't see what I can do about it. The law must take its course."

"Suppose she were put out of harm's way? In a well run old people's Home, for instance?"

Inspector Chambers took a few moments to answer, then said slowly, "It's possible. I could put it to the Commissioner, and he could write to the Minister."

"There's a long waiting list for most

of the Homes for the elderly but I think I could get her into the Sundown Shelter. It's not as popular as the others because it's run on a strict routine. The matron's most efficient but she's also a bit of a martinet and believes in firm discipline of both staff and inmates. The place is kept spotlessly clean and the residents very well fed and cared for, as long as they don't step out of line."

"Well . . . I could try . . . "

"Miss Wallace's death could surely be recorded as an accident. It *was* an accident — all right, accidental murder, if you like."

"It might be possible," conceded Trevor. "The Police Department is not inhuman and it would save us a lot of work and expense."

"Can you spare time to come and see her? To hear her own version of what she did? I think you'd realise that incarceration would be unnecessary public expenditure. Her own income and her national superannuation would pay for lodging in a decent, registered Home, such as the one I mentioned, where she could come to no harm and do none."

"I'll have to get a statement from her, whatever they decide. Yes, I can come right now if you like. Will she be home?"

"It's nearly five o'clock, so she's almost sure to be. She never goes out in the evening."

"All right. Better to take her by surprise than to phone first. I'll pick up a constable and order a car. You'd better come too, if you don't mind. She might clam up and refuse to talk or else deny the whole thing."

But Mrs Dibbett was quite happy to talk. She welcomed them all and offered them tea, appearing disappointed when they refused. Then she told them all about it. "He was a very bad man, you see. It was best that he didn't live any more." She looked at the vicar and went on, "Well, I thought so then. Mr Jarrett has pointed out to me that it was wrong of me to poison his mug. *Thou shalt not kill*, you know. It had just slipped my mind at the time." Yes, she had gone into the public library in the end she found a section in one book headed *Ceramic Toxicology* and it mentioned a poison that Mr Solley actually had in a jar. He'd shown it to her and the jar was labelled. Very quick, he'd said, so it wouldn't hurt, would it? Though being stabbed in the back wouldn't hurt for long either, would it? She did hope not. She didn't like anyone to suffer. Then when Mr Solley was out at his kiln she had simply gone into his studio and helped herself — not the whole jar, of course, just enough for her purpose. And Mr Clagg's door was always unlocked and he was often out. It was really very simple.

She kept looking up at the ceiling. "I wonder what's going on up there? I think some of them are having an argument. Did you know that the barium given in hospital before X-rays is the only form of barium which is not poisonous? Most interesting. Oh dear, what a noise they're making. Or perhaps it's just Mr Fuller. He does Physical exercises from a book you know."

Inspector Chambers said, "You do realise, Mrs Dibbett, that Constable Warrington is taking down what you say and then you'll be asked to read and sign the final statement?"

"Why, of course, inspector. You told me he would and you said I need not answer any questions if I preferred not to. Don't you remember? But of course I don't mind answering . . . oh, that was rather loud, wasn't it?" She looked up again at the ceiling. "Quite a thump. They must be moving the furniture around. It's not usually noisy here. I'll be sorry to leave if the house is sold. Do you think . . . ?"

And then a woman screamed.

All three men rushed out the door and started up the stairs. Mary Grayson was coming down, agitatedly flapping her hands. "Quick, hurry," she gasped.

"Denis Day is trying to kill Hugh."

Hugh's door was open. They saw him standing in the middle of the room, alert, on guard, ready to fend off an attack. He had picked up a table knife but was unable to reach Denis, who was holding a chair up in front of him. The inspector was the first to hasten into the room. But too late. Even as he ran through the door, Denis Day brought down the chair on Hugh's head. Hugh fell heavily on the brass fender, rolled over once and then lay motionless.

Denis slowly put the chair down and turned to face them. Mary was in the room now, staring horrified at the scene. Inspector Chambers knelt down by Hugh, put a hand on his chest, pulled back an eyelid. "He's alive," he muttered. Then he got to his feet and looked at Denis. "Mr Day . . . "

Mary ran across to Hugh but the constable blocked her way. She fought to get past him, "Let me go to him.

Oh Hugh, Hugh!"

The inspector ignored her. "Mr Day, would you please take Miss Grayson downstairs?" Mary turned, then cowered, trembling white, against the wall. She raised a finger and pointed it shakily at Denis. "No, No! You don't understand. He's the . . . He mur . . . mur . . . murd . . . "

Jabal strode over to her and put his hands on her shoulders. "Mary, look at me!" When her eyes slowly turned to meet his, he said gently, "Go down with Denis. He'll look after you. He has murdered no one. From what I know of Denis Day, I doubt if he would intentionally kill even an ant."

14

IT was Mary Grayson who answered the doorbell at Fairway Flats, "Oh, Hullo, Mr Jarrett. Come in. You were right. He doesn't. He never has. He told me. How did you know?"

Mary was flushed, animated, her eyes sparkling, and she looked unusually pretty.

"Could you be a little more explicit, my dear? Who doesn't what?"

"Denis. He doesn't even kill ants. Like you said. He wipes up all food crumbs so they don't come in and he says they have as much right to live as he has and one just has to take precautions to see they do their living outside a house and not in it."

Jabal smiled at her. "I approve his view. And I gather you do, too?"

"Oh *yes*! of *course*! He's so . . . oh, he's absolutely super, Mr Jarrett, he really is. I always liked him but I didn't realise how much. I don't know how *you* knew he was so nice. I suppose you get used to summing people up in your job. And he likes me awfully too. In fact, he and I . . . " She stopped, breathless.

"I'm delighted to hear it," said Jabal.

"We've found a place with an aunt of one of the girls in Fabrics. Her aunt wants to let the back part of her house and she's had a kitchen and a bathroom put in and there's even a bit of a garden. Isn't that fabulous? And we're going to get *married*! I bet that surprises you."

"I'm pleased."

"It's something different, you see. Everyone's going de facto these days and I think we ought to show the world that we're not going to be pressurised into conforming. Den says that's Hugh's influence still hanging over me but if that's what I want, that's what we'll do and he'd have liked to get married anyway, whether it was the thing to do or not."

"Good. A church wedding?"

"Well, no. We're having it done at the Registry Office. I hope you don't mind?"

"I am not at all offended on behalf of the Church. The choice is entirely your own. I'm glad you have sufficient faith in the solidity of your affection for each other to make the tie legally binding, and I wish you every happiness. I came to see Mrs Dibbett. Do you know if she's in?"

"Yes, I think she's there, but won't you come and say hullo to Denis first? I was just going up myself. Oh do come. Just for a few minutes?"

"I'll be glad to. Lead the way."

Denis did not look as happy as Mary. He greeted Jabal, invited him into his room and offered him a chair. Then he said gloomily, "Hugh Fuller is dead. Did you know?"

"Yes," Jabal told him. "Before he died he confessed to killing Tom Solley. He said he had not intended to but another fight developed and got out of hand. I'm inclined to believe what he said."

"But *I* killed *him*, I *killed* him."

"You delivered a blow in self-defence. That blow caused him to fall and the fall was fatal because he struck his head on the corner of the fender. The pathologist has reported that death was due to that impact and not to the blow with the chair."

"How does he know?"

"I didn't ask for details. I think it's something to do with depth of the wound and amount of bleeding. But I assure you that if Government pathologists issue a statement such as that, one does not question it. They are cautious scientific experts and have good grounds for any conclusion they come to."

"I still killed him, because I made him fall."

"You were defending yourself," said Mary. "You *had* to hit him."

"I suppose so," said Denis doubtfully.

"He was coming at me with a knife. He seemed almost demented, out of his mind. I'd never seen him quite like it. But I roused his temper, so it was my fault."

"Why didn't Cecil Martin come and help you? He must have heard the row."

"Thank heaven he didn't. If he had it would've been to help Hugh, not me. I guess he was cowering in his room frightened of *me*. As soon as I'd got upstairs that day he came out babbling about going to church and church bells and accused me of lying and therefore murdering Clagg, Josie and Tom. I was so taken aback and so angry and being a bit worked up because I was thinking of accusing Hugh of the same thing . . . well, I'm afraid I lost my cool. I told him to go to hell or he'd be the fourth victim. He scuttled back into his flat and I heard him lock the door."

"It was rather brave of him to accuse you," said Mary.

"I agree," said Jabal. "The effort will have done him good and given him a little more confidence." He thought back to young Charlie Simmons, who had altered the hymn numbers.

Denis went on, "Well, I went in to see Hugh, feeling really angry. I told him you'd said he wanted to ask me something — what was it? It was for more money, of course. Then I told him off. One word led to another and you know what happened. I killed the poor fellow."

Jabal said, "You must stop blaming yourself. Inspector Chambers has been talking to me about what he calls non-culpable homicide and provocation and such like. The gist of it is that you'll probably not even be charged with manslaughter. In a way it was the police themselves who killed him."

"What do you mean?"

"The police confiscated from each of you any drugs or medicaments which might be mislabelled, disguised poison. Aspirin, disinfectant . . . the inspector gave me a list of them. I wasn't sure why, so I did some research. A substance called stelazine was found in Fuller's flat, in the form of blue tablets. The constable confiscated it but left him the repeat, rightly so, as it was a prescribed medicament. But Hugh neglected to get a repeat. I hadn't heard of the substance but when I looked it up in a medical encyclopedia I learned that it is prescribed for manic depressives to keep their condition under control. Without it, their psychosis may be activated and the patient may switch to a manic phase. Medical records are normally confidential but after death they may be released to the police and I think Hugh's mental condition will be confirmed." He looked at Denis. "I . . . er . . . I used that encyclopedia to look up *all* the drugs on the list."

"It's all right," said Denis. "I've told her. Mary knows I'm an epileptic." He was more cheerful now.

"As though *I'd* mind," said Mary. "That's why he was always so quiet and reserved, thinking no one would like him if they knew. He's not a bit stuffy, Mr Jarrett. I didn't really know him before."

"You didn't know how stupid I can be in an emergency," said Denis. "I behaved like an idiot when I found poor old Tom. I'd never met violent death before. It was ghastly sight. I tried to keep calm and I did all the wrong things. And as for the church bells — I really thought that would mean it was eleven o'clock."

"There are certain advantages in going to church," laughed Jabal.

"And I dithered and behaved like an imbecile. It must've been about a quarter to eleven that I went in and found him. It seemed a long time before I rang the police, but when you're upset and confused . . . "

"Of course," Mary assured him. "*I* think you behaved wonderfully."

"What a fool I was! No wonder the police suspected me."

"You are wrong," Jabal told him.

"Everyone came under suspicion for Miss Wallace's death, but it was obvious from the first that you were innocent of Solley's. It has now been accepted that Clagg was killed, and his flat wrecked, by a street gang. And Miss Wallace . . . by accident."

"What sort of accident?"

That was something Jabal did not intend to disclose. He answered, "She used a mug in which poison had been left," then went on quickly, "Hugh told the police that he thought Solley had poisoned her, went in to have a talk to him and one of their fights started up. I think he was speaking the truth. Dying men generally do. He was presumably in a manic phase when he saw Solley. He accused him of poisoning Miss Wallace, an argument developed and Hugh lost control. The police suspected him from the first but couldn't connect him with the other two deaths. I, too, thought him the most likely person here to have killed a fellow tenant. If you remember, I went up to his room when I first met you all and talked with him for some time. I was for three years chaplain at Kingstone Mental Hospital and I recognised certain symptoms of mental abnormality."

"But why did you say they didn't suspect me?" asked Denis. "They must've known I was wrong about the church bells."

"I certainly pointed it out," Jabal told him, and your delay in informing the police was suspicious but they knew you were innocent because you picked up the mallet."

"I thought that would clinch my guilt. I was expecting to be arrested any day, because I'd left my fingerprints on it. It was another stupid thing to do, picking it up in a sort of daze when I saw the blood on it. However could that show I *didn't* kill him?"

"You picked it up delicately, gingerly, didn't you? Your fingerprints were clear, imposed on all others, and in such a position to show that you could not possibly have held the mallet in that manner while delivering a heavy blow."

Denis laughed. "And all the time I thought I was chief suspect. I was to Mary, anyway. I'm marrying a girl who suspected me of murdering three persons. What a story to tell our grandchildren."

"Oh Denis, are we going to have grandchildren?"

"Lots of them. Won't it sound good in their morning talks at school? 'Granny thought Grandad had killed three people, so she married him.'"

"It was only at the last that I thought you'd done it, Denis. Why did you lie about your quarrel with Tom?"

"I didn't lie, you ninny."

"You told us Tom struck out at you with a knife. But Tom was left-handed so I worked out he would've hit you on the right temple, not the left."

It was Jabal who answered, "He also told me, Mary, that Tom didn't even stop his work to do it. Adding the final touches to a large jardiniere must be a delicate task, requiring a firm, sure touch. He'd naturally use his master hand for the job. It was with his right that he absently picked up a knife and lashed out and because he was left-handed he was as clumsy with it as most of us are with our left. I doubt that he meant to strike Denis at all. It was just a threatening gesture. Am I right Denis?"

"Yes, I think you are. Finding he had actually nicked me was what made him so cross at the time. But he wasn't the sort to apologise."

"You never told us what you were arguing about," said Mary.

"He said you envied Josie's large earnings and implied you might be thinking of changing your profession. So I lost my temper and called him some rude names."

"Oh, Denis, how *nice* of you!"

The two men laughed and Denis changed the subject. "Did you ever find out who altered that land agent's sign, Mr Jarrett? Who had the cheek to write 'Coffin to Let'?"

"We don't know. Probably just a passing student, as we thought at the time. Things are so often exactly what they seem and we bring unnecessary complications in our explanations for them. Clagg's death, for instance. The police were convinced it was the work of intruding vandals. It was only the ensuing deaths that made them doubt the obvious."

Denis said, "But four deaths in one house is a bit of a coincidence, isn't it?"

"It was not coincidence. It was a chain of events, one leading to another." To explain fully would involve telling them of Mrs Dibbett's part in it, so he went on quickly, "The police tell me that this house is being sold and the buyer wants vacant possession. I'm very glad you two have somewhere to go."

"And the Martins have a flat, too," Mary told him. "The Inspector put them onto it. Wasn't it decent of him? And Vera went round to see it. I think she made a better impression than Cecil would've and what with the Inspector's recommendation, they actually got it. Cecil's started to grow a beard because of your advice."

"I have never advised anyone to grow a beard," Jabal protested.

"Well, it was because of what you said. And Daphne's going up to Kaikohe to join a sort of commune. Oh, and the Inspector said he might be able to get Cecil a job. He *is* nice, isn't he? I suppose they have to seem horrible to frighten people into confessing if they can. But what's going to happen to poor Mrs Dibbett? She doesn't really want to go and live with one of her sons. All her interests are up here."

"I think we can get her into a Home if she'll consent to go," said Jabal. "That's what I came to see her about and I'd better go and do it. My best wishes to you both. *Whoso findeth a wife, findeth a good thing.*"

"Oh, did Paul say that too?"

"No, Paul said *It is better to marry than to burn.*" He left them to make sense of that. Scholars had been trying for centuries. Then he went downstairs to see Mrs Dibbett.

He hoped to heaven that she would consent to enter the Sundown Shelter. If so, no charges would be laid. Trevor had manged to arrange that. It would be cruel to tell a woman of seventy-eight that she had been responsible for three deaths, and it would help no one. Jabal knew her to be kind, generous, and in many respects tolerant and understanding. As long as she was in an institution where she could do no harm and come to no harm, she would be permitted to finish out her life in peace. The Sundown Shelter was not the Home Jabal would have chosen but it had a vacancy and she would be safe there. The matron, Miss Hardcastle, was severe, too severe in Jabal's opinion. She lacked understanding of the elderly and had no sympathy with their desire to be idle or to spend hours dozing in an easy chair in front of television soaps. She maintained that constant activity and exercise would prolong their life and she could be right. She was devoted to her job, she nursed her charges well and watched conscientiously over their safety and health. Her ideas of what was good for them did not accord with their own, but Mrs Dibbett would at least be well looked after. And Miss Hardcastle was an ambitious woman. She would very likely be moving on soon to a larger Home and a more responsible position.

Mrs Dibbett was pleased to see Jabal but she looked a little worried. "The house is to be sold, vicar, did you know?"

"Yes, Mrs Dibbett. That's what I came to see you about. There happens to be a vacancy in the Sundown Shelter."

Mrs Dibbett shook her head vigorously. "Oh, no, vicar. I'll never go

302

there. It's a terrible place. It's the matron, you know. Miss Hardheart or something. Poor Lucy Comfrey's there and I've been to see her and she's told me all about it. That woman makes her life a misery."

"I have other parishioners there, Mrs Dibbett. The food is good, the rooms are kept clean, there's a large lounge with coloured television . . ."

Mrs Dibbett waved aside all these amenities. "I know all that. But that matron, vicar! That *woman*! Do you know she won't allow smoking in the bedrooms?"

"You don't smoke."

"No, but some of the elderly men do. And one lady wanted to keep a cat. That's all. Just a small, harmless cat. And she wasn't allowed to. That *woman* said it was unhygienic."

"She makes many concessions. She encourages activities of all sorts. I believe they have a barbecue once a fortnight in the summer and picnics at the beach."

"And she forces them all to attend. Lucy Comfrey says it's *supposed* to be optional but if they don't go they're in disgrace and *she* says they must be off colour and puts them on a special diet without fat. Oh, it's just terrible there, vicar. I wouldn't dream of going myself. Never, never!"

Confound the woman. It was either a Home or a prison cell. Jabal made another effort. "I admit she's strict but it's in the residents' own interests. She's only the matron. There are other staff. And she won't be there for ever."

"No," said Mrs Dibbett. "No, I suppose not." A dreamy expression came into her eyes and she looked out the window. She hadn't thought of that. Of course, she needn't be there for ever. She needn't be there much longer at all. One could free all those poor souls. A barbecue once a fortnight, he'd said. One would have to be careful . . . couldn't have anyone else affected. But . . . yes, with care it could be arranged. And it would be such a *useful* thing to do. Really, a public service. And quite painless.

She turned back to the vicar. "A barbecue once a fortnight, you said? Does the matron do that herself?"

"Yes, she organises it all herself."

"And cooks the food on it?"

"Yes. She's a very energetic lady, just as you are yourself, Mrs Dibbett. You should get on very well together."

"There are spacious grounds, aren't there?"

"Indeed yes, most attractive." Was she weakening? His hopes rose.

"Plenty of shrubs?"

"Yes. May varieties. Park-like grounds." She *was* giving in. Thank the Lord.

"Are there any oleanders?"

"Certainly there. You like oleanders? I saw some magnificent specimens last time I was there. They're actually coming into bloom at present."

The old lady's face cleared and to her tired old eyes came a gleam of happy anticipation. She smiled demurely and said, "Very well, vicar. Thank you for all your trouble. I'll be happy to accept the vacancy."

THE END

A FOOT IN THE GRAVE
Bruce Marshall

About to be imprisoned and tortured in Buenos Aires, John Smith escapes, only to become involved in an aeroplane hijacking.

DEAD TROUBLE
Martin Carroll

Trespassing brought Jennifer Denning more than she bargained for. She was totally unprepared for the violence which was to lie in her path.

HOURS TO KILL
Ursula Curtiss

Margaret went to New Mexico to look after her sick sister's rented house and felt a sharp edge of fear when the absent landlady arrived.

THE DEATH OF ABBE DIDIER
Richard Grayson

Inspector Gautier of the Sûreté investigates three crimes which are strangely connected.

NIGHTMARE TIME
Hugh Pentecost

Have the missing major and his wife met with foul play somewhere in the Beaumont Hotel, or is their disappearance a carefully planned step in an act of treason?

BLOOD WILL OUT
Margaret Carr

Why was the manor house so oddly familiar to Elinor Howard? Who would have guessed that a Sunday School outing could lead to murder?

THE DRACULA MURDERS
Philip Daniels

The Horror Ball was interrupted by a spectral figure who warned the merrymakers they were tampering with the unknown.

THE LADIES
OF LAMBTON GREEN
Liza Shepherd

Why did murdered Robin Colquhoun's picture pose such a threat to the ladies of Lambton Green?

CARNABY
AND THE GAOLBREAKERS
Peter N. Walker

Detective Sergeant James Aloysius Carnaby-King is sent to prison as bait. When he joins in an escape he is thrown headfirst into a vicious murder hunt.

MUD IN HIS EYE
Gerald Hammond

The harbourmaster's body is found mangled beneath Major Smyle's yacht. What is the sinister significance of the illicit oysters?

THE SCAVENGERS
Bill Knox

Among the masses of struggling fish in the *Tecta*'s nets was a larger, darker, ominously motionless form . . . the body of a skin diver.

DEATH IN ARCADY
Stella Phillips

Detective Inspector Matthew Furnival works unofficially with the local police when a brutal murder takes place in a caravan camp.

STORM CENTRE
Douglas Clark

Detective Chief Superintendent Masters, temporarily lecturing in a police staff college, finds there's more to the job than a few weeks relaxation in a rural setting.

THE MANUSCRIPT MURDERS
Roy Harley Lewis

Antiquarian bookseller Matthew Coll, acquires a rare 16th century manuscript. But when the Dutch professor who had discovered the journal is murdered, Coll begins to doubt its authenticity.

SHARENDEL
Margaret Carr

Ruth didn't want all that money. And she didn't want Aunt Cass to die. But at Sharendel things looked different. She began to wonder if she had a split personality.

MURDER TO BURN
Laurie Mantell

Sergeants Steven Arrow and Lance Brendon, of the New Zealand police force, come upon a woman's body in the water. When the dead woman is identified they begin to realise that they are investigating a complex fraud.

YOU CAN HELP ME
Maisie Birmingham

Whilst running the Citizens' Advice Bureau, Kate Weatherley is attacked with no apparent motive. Then the body of one of her clients is found in her room.

DAGGERS DRAWN
Margaret Carr

Stacey Manston was the kind of girl who could take most things in her stride, but three murders were something different . . .

THE MONTMARTRE MURDERS
Richard Grayson

Inspector Gautier of Sûreté investigates the disappearance of artist Théo, the heir to a fortune.

GRIZZLY TRAIL
Gwen Moffat

Miss Pink, alone in the Rockies, helps in a search for missing hikers, solves two cruel murders and has the most terrifying experience of her life when she meets a grizzly bear!

BLINDMAN'S BLUFF
Margaret Carr

Kate Deverill had considered suicide. It was one way out — and preferable to being murdered.